Total Surrender

Total Surrender

C. McCray

St. Martin's Griffin
New York

TOTAL SURRENDER. Copyright © 2009 by Cheyenne McCray.
All rights reserved. Printed in the United States of America.
For information, address St. Martin's Press,
175 Fifth Avenue, New York, N.Y. 10010.

www.stmartins.com

LIBRARY OF CONGRESS CATALOGING-IN-PUBLICATION DATA

McCray, Cheyenne.
    Total surrender / Cheyenne McCray.—1st ed.
        p.   cm.
    ISBN-13: 978-0-312-53754-8
    ISBN-10: 0-312-53754-9
    I. Title.
    PS3613.C38634T67   2009
    813'.6—dc22

                                                    2008033592

First Edition: March 2009

10 9 8 7 6 5 4 3 2 1

To the awesome ladies at CheysFantasies chat group. You rock!

www.groups.yahoo.com/group/Cheys_Fantasies/

To my readers

Enjoy this foray into the world of the erotic and dare to indulge in your deepest sexual fantasies.

Bondage. Domination. Submission.

Dare.

Author's Note

A version of the following three novellas was originally published with a small e-publisher in a collection titled *Erotic Interludes*.

Seduction isn't making someone do what they don't want to do. Seduction is enticing someone into doing what they secretly want to do already. —*Waiter Rant Weblog*

Sweet Surrender

Chapter 1

With a sigh of longing, Sheila Lane placed her elbow on her desk, propped her chin on her hand, and studied Adamo Tassoni as he spoke with one of the company's Vice Presidents. The two men were engrossed in conversation, unaware of her soulful expression.

Thank God. She'd die on the spot if Mr. Tassoni could read on her face how much she wanted him.

How much she loved him.

Not that it mattered now. She still couldn't believe it. Adam was leaving. The CEO, President, and owner of Tassoni Investments had sold the company and was turning over the reins to Edward Johnson, effective today.

After three years of being Adam's personal assistant, Sheila found herself with a new boss.

And the man she'd fallen in love with years ago would be walking out of her life . . . forever.

Not that he'd ever been less than professional with her. Not that he'd ever shown the slightest inclination that he might be interested in her personally.

On occasion he'd given her smiles of approval that had melted her heart, but that was it. Sometimes he'd lean over her shoulder to review her notes and she would almost moan out loud at the feel of his warm breath against her neck. When she'd hand him a document or a file, her fingers would lightly brush his and she'd feel a jolt of electricity from the roots of her hair to her toenails. But Adam never gave any sign that he'd felt anything at all.

Sheila sighed again as she continued to study his profile. Of course she likely wasn't his type, although she'd never met any woman he might be dating. Sheila was petite in height and had breasts so large she'd topple over if she didn't have a nice-sized ass to keep her stable. She kept her wheat blond hair pulled back in a clip, and she wore conservative business suits when she was in the office. She was working class . . . he was a god.

Sicilian by birth, Adamo had lived in the United States most of his life. He still had the sexiest accent, and when he spoke, her nipples went hard automatically and only her business suits kept him from seeing the taut buds peak against the soft fabric of her blouses. The man was a good six feet tall, with broad, powerful shoulders. He was built like a pro basketball player, lean and muscular. A man built for speed . . . and sex.

So many times she'd imagined what it would feel like to be taken by Adam. Whether it was hard and rough, or slow and sensual, all her fantasies revolved around him. And all her fantasies involved him dominating her, mastering her like he mastered everything else in his business and in his life.

Like right now, as she watched him, she wondered what it would feel like to be on her knees before him, his trousers undone and his erection jutting out in front of her. Her wrists would be tied behind her and his hand on the back of her head, forcing her to go down on his cock. She'd swirl her tongue around the head and then take him deep, to the back of her throat.

She clenched her thighs together at the thought and her clit ached as she imagined how he'd pump his hips against her face as he held her captive.

At that moment Adam cast a look at Sheila. Her cheeks flamed, and she felt like she could sink through the floor with embarrassment at being caught staring at him and fantasizing about him.

She quickly moved her hand from her chin to the file in front of her and dropped her gaze to the papers she was supposed to be going through. She felt the heat of his stare and hoped her face wasn't as red as it felt. After three years she should be an expert at hiding her feelings for the man.

While she pretended to study the file, she listened to his powerful voice, and she almost teared up at the thought of never hearing that throbbing tone again. Her thoughts wandered and she imagined him taking her on his polished mahogany desk, her wrists tied above her head, his hands and mouth upon her body, and his cock sliding into her wet channel—

"Sheila?"

Her head shot up at the sound of Adam's voice so close to her, and her pulse pounded in her ears. He was standing beside her desk and studying her with the intense aquamarine eyes that gave away his Sicilian heritage. The heady, masculine scent of him surrounded her, a combination of his light aftershave and the smell of pure male.

"Are you all right?" he asked in that deep, penetrating voice that made her shiver.

Sheila cleared her throat and nodded. "Yes, Mr. Tassoni." A very large part of her wanted to beg him to take her with him, wherever he was going. Hell, just to *take* her.

But she kept herself under control. "It's been a pleasure serving you these past three years. I—I—" She faltered, wanting to say, *I'm going to miss you.* Instead she said, "I wish you well in your future endeavors." Her cheeks went hotter at the lameness of her words.

God, she was so pitiful.

A flicker of something crossed Adam's features and he gave a slow nod. "It has certainly been a pleasure, Sheila." He paused, those gorgeous eyes never letting hers go. "You have been a most . . . efficient assistant."

Sheila's heart plummeted and she attempted to keep her voice steady. "Thank you, Mr. Tassoni."

He didn't even grace her with one of his rare smiles. He simply turned away and strode into his office.

One last time.

Adam shut the heavy mahogany door behind him and raked his fingers through his black hair as he ordered his cock to stand down. He wore his slacks loose because the beautiful Sheila Lane would invariably make him rock-hard with one demure glance, with one whiff of her light orange-blossom perfume.

Oh, he'd recognized those glances for what they were, and although he'd wanted to take advantage of the delectable Miss Lane, he didn't believe in crossing the employer/employee line. He never mixed business with pleasure.

Even though what he wanted from Sheila went beyond pleasure.

Well now there was nothing to stop him.

In a few strides he reached the floor-to-ceiling windows of his luxurious office and stared out at the Los Angeles skyline. The sky was a cloudless cerulean blue and a light wind caused palm fronds to wave to and fro below the ten-story office building. Tassoni Investments occupied the entire top floor. What had been a venture capital start-up company had just sold for millions, and now Adam was free to move on to new and more interesting ventures.

Including the blond beauty who had been his assistant for three years. For three years she had taunted him with her fine ass and luscious breasts, even though most of the time she'd hidden them beneath form-fitting suits. Occasionally she would take off her jacket, and when she moved he would catch a glimpse of the curve of one breast through gaps in her conservative button-up blouse.

And that ass of hers. Often he had pictured her on all fours as he slid his cock into her slick core and spanked those cheeks until they were a fine shade of pink. As pink as her face had just turned when he'd caught her watching him.

But it was more than that. More than the desire to have sex with Sheila. From the time he hired her she'd penetrated his soul straight to his heart. It had been unexpected, but increased with every moment, every day he had worked with her. It had been so fucking difficult to maintain a professional distance when he'd wanted to take her in his arms and have her every way a man could have a woman.

Every way.

Andi Kelly, one of Tassoni's three VPs, braced one hand on the copy machine as she watched Sheila making several copies of a document. Andi and Sheila had hit it off at one of the company Christmas parties when Sheila first started at Tassoni Investments.

"Girl, you've got to get over Tassoni," Andi said. "That or proposition him."

"Humph." Sheila turned her gaze to the copier and watched the incandescent light flash with every copy the machine made. Her eyes were glazed and her heart heavy. "Three years, Andi." Sheila fidgeted with the top button at the throat of her blouse. "And all I could say was 'I wish you well in your future endeavors.' How lame is that?"

Andi snorted. "Well, honey, it was better than throwing yourself at his feet and begging him to take you right on the Berber carpeting in his office." Sheila cast her friend a glance as Andi continued, "Although that certainly would have caught his attention."

Sheila rolled her eyes and Andi added, "*I* would've asked him out for a drink."

The copier stopped, and Sheila snatched out the original and grabbed the copies. "You've got guts. I'm just a wimp, plain and simple."

Andi shook her head, her long black hair sliding over her shoulders like a silken curtain. "You've got to stop playing it safe and take chances. *Live*, girlfriend."

"I'm not you." Sheila strode out of the copy room toward her desk. "Besides, it's too late. He already left."

"It's never too late," Andi shot back as she rounded her cubicle and vanished from sight, just as Sheila almost smacked into Kate Baron, Vice President and resident Bitch from Hell.

Kate smirked and raised a perfectly plucked eyebrow. "Adamo Tassoni wouldn't waste his time with you."

Sheila's cheeks burned as she moved behind her desk and eased into her chair. "I don't know what you're talking about."

"Oh, I think you do." Kate laughed, a fake, cultured laugh that grated on Sheila's nerves. Kate propped a perfectly manicured hand on her perfectly slim hip. "After all this time I'd think you would have realized that the last person he would be interested in is you. All these years you've made it only too obvious that you want him. And it's only too obvious he wants nothing to do with you. Except maybe a fuck if you do throw yourself at him."

Sheila's face burned hotter as she realized Kate must have been listening outside the copy room. "Is there anything I can do for you, *Ms. Baron?*"

The woman brushed a piece of imaginary lint from the sleeve of her perfectly tailored black suit. "Don't waste his time any further by making a fool of yourself."

With that the Wicked Witch of West LA turned and strode down the hall, presumably toward her own elegant office.

Sheila slid into her seat and clenched the copies in her hand. *Bitch, bitch, bitch!*

She moved her gaze to Adam's empty office. Next week the movers would bring Edward Johnson's belongings into the luxurious office and she would officially be his assistant.

Kate's words burned in her ears and she longed for a cotton swab to clean them right out. Rather than discourage her from contacting Adam, Kate's digs only pissed Sheila off.

Andi was right. She should contact Adam. She had his cell number and his home number. It wouldn't hurt a damn bit to ask him out for a drink. They'd been coworkers long enough that she could simply say she'd like to get together for a farewell drink. If it led to more . . .

She stuffed the copies into a file folder and grabbed the cordless phone receiver before her nerves and self-doubt got the better of her. With shaking fingers she dialed Adam's cell number, a number she'd memorized long ago. Just as the phone started to ring, she spotted something propped up against a picture of her family.

It was an envelope with *Sheila* embossed in gold across the creamy white surface.

She dropped the receiver back onto its cradle and picked up the envelope. It was thick and heavy, obviously expensive stationery. Curiosity filled her as she turned it over. Gold wax sealed the envelope with a crest she didn't recognize. She broke the seal, slowly opened the envelope, and pulled out a single sheet of paper of the same heavy stationery. The paper was folded in half and, when she opened it, her heart began to pound.

Across the white surface a single word was embossed in gold: *Tonight.*

Chapter 2

All the way home Sheila's mind raced and her pulse pounded in her ears. She barely kept her mind on traffic and her little Nissan in its own lane. When she reached her condo, she parked in the garage, snatched her purse off the passenger seat, and slowly went into the small house through the garage door.

Okay, nothing to get excited over, her calm, rational mind told her. *It might be nothing at all.*

The door banged shut behind her and she faced the tiny but cozy living room. "It could just be a party someone's holding," she said aloud.

"Who's throwing a party?"

At the sound of Greg's voice, Sheila nearly jumped out of her skin. She held her purse tight to her chest and glared at her roommate, who'd come up behind her. "I've told you a zillion times not to sneak up on me like that."

Greg gave her an unrepentant grin. "But it's so much fun."

"Get lost, surfer boy." Sheila turned her back on her too-cute-for-his-own-good friend and slipped into her bedroom.

Of course surfer boy followed her. "C'mon, give."

She set her purse on her vanity and tossed her suit jacket onto the bed. "It's Friday night. Don't you have a beach-volleyball-bonfire thing to go to?"

He hitched his shoulder against the door frame. "So what's up?"

"I told you there's no party." Sheila pulled her hair clip out and let her long hair tumble over her shoulders. "Now beat it." She began unbuttoning her up-to-the-neck blouse in front of Greg. They'd been friends for so long that neither of them worried much about modesty in front of the other. As long as they had underwear on, what difference did it make?

Greg cocked an eyebrow as she slid out of her blouse. "You really should get rid of those granny bras and panties. Get something really hot from Victoria's Secret or Frederick's of Hollywood."

Sheila gave him a glare as she shimmied out of her past-the-knee skirt and flung it onto the bed with everything else. "Like anyone's going to see them but you. And you don't count."

"The only reason you haven't dated is because you've been lusting over one man and won't give anyone else a chance." He tossed wavy sun-streaked hair from his eyes and his voice grew softer. "So, was it hard with him leaving today?"

With a heavy sigh, Sheila peeled her nylons over her ample hips and down to her ankles where she stepped out of them. "It's hard to believe that I won't see him again."

"You should call him." Greg's expression was serious. "The man can't be blind. You're caring, sensitive, and, well, you're pretty."

She smiled. "You're just saying that because you want me to spring for dinner tonight."

The corner of his mouth quirked. "Well there's that," he responded with a wink, then his expression went back to serious. "Call him. What can it hurt?"

"You sound like Andi." Sheila studied her reflection in the vanity. Her bra was heavy-duty and held up her large breasts, but didn't show them to their full advantage. And she had to admit the cotton panties were a bit on the grandma-ish side. "Actually, I did start to call him, but then I found something on my desk."

She didn't know why she was telling Greg, other than the fact that he'd been her best friend and confidant since high school, when they were both fifteen. And here it was, sixteen years later, and they were living together, unattached and no serious prospects in either of their futures. Although Greg played the field, he never stayed with one girl for long.

They were truly pathetic.

"Well . . . what was it?" Keen interest lit Greg's warm brown eyes.

Sheila went to her purse, slipped out the envelope, and handed it to Greg.

A puzzled expression crossed his features and then he whistled. His gaze shot to hers, and he tossed the envelope and paper onto her bureau. "I'll bet it has something to do with the package."

Before Sheila could ask "What package?" Greg tore out of the room. In a few moments he came back bearing a thick white box bound with a gold bow. A single long-stemmed red rose had been slipped through the bow.

He handed the package to her. "Some guy dropped this off about fifteen minutes before you got home."

Sheila's hands trembled with a combination of uncertainty, fear, and excitement as she took the box from him. After she set it on her vanity, she pulled the red rose from the bow and brought it to her nose. She inhaled the sweet scent, drawing it in and letting it seep through her being.

Greg punched her lightly in the arm. "Hurry up already."

With nervous anticipation, she set the rose aside and pulled at the bow until it fell away, and then she lifted the lid from the box and tossed it aside, and caught her breath. On a bed of sapphire blue satin was another creamy envelope with her name embossed in gold.

More quickly now she broke the seal and pulled out the heavy paper. It simply read, "7:00 P.M."

Greg snatched the paper from her fingers and let out another low whistle. But Sheila was too intent on exploring the contents of the box. She withdrew the blue satin and discovered that it was a strapless gown, simple yet elegant—although it looked like it would barely cover her breasts and was a little too short, even by her petite standards. Carefully she laid the dress on her bed beside her discarded work clothing, then returned to the box.

Inside it were an evening bag that matched the dress to perfection, a lovely strapless sapphire blue bra, thong underwear, a garter belt, and sheer thigh-high stockings.

With every item she withdrew, Sheila's cheeks grew hotter and hotter. "Oh my God," she said as she brought out a dainty pair of three-inch-heeled sandals. Everything looked perfectly sized, as though the person knew her intimately.

"Shit." Greg tossed the second note on top of the first one. "The guy's got class, I'll say that."

Sheila turned her gaze to him. "I'm supposed to dress up in all this and be ready at seven for a man I don't even know?"

Greg shrugged. "I'd say it's obvious he knows you *very* well."

"A stalker?"

He rolled his eyes.

"Not your friends Devon or Terry?"

"Hell no." Greg laughed. "They haven't got class enough to send a woman a box of chocolates, much less go through all this trouble."

Sheila's mind kept going back to Adamo Tassoni. "He wouldn't, would he?" she asked herself aloud.

"Ding!" Greg made his voice sound like a game-show host's. "Sheila Lane, if you're talking about your mega-rich ex-boss, you're tonight's winner."

"Wow." She shook her head slowly. "I mean, no. He hasn't given me any reason, *ever*, to believe he'd do anything like this."

"He has plenty of reasons, but I'm not going to go into them now." Greg glanced at the clock on her bureau. "You've got less than an hour to hop in the shower and be ready in time."

Sheila gripped the shoes tighter. "I can't just jump because someone sends me a couple of notes and a box of clothes."

Greg backed out through her doorway and grabbed the door handle. "Time to stop playing it safe and take a chance, hon," he said as he shut the door behind him.

She stuck her tongue out and glared at the door. Yeah, he and Andi would get along just fine.

Fifty-five minutes later, Sheila was dressed and ready. She stood in front of the mirror again, this time amazed at the transformation in her appearance. The sapphire satin clung to her curves and plunged low enough to show her generous cleavage. The lacy bra, thong, and garters felt sensual and wanton, and the high heels made her feel extremely sexy. She'd put her hair up, but this time in a soft and elegant look instead of the usual business style she used at work.

Everything had been a perfect fit. As if the man knew her better than she knew herself.

Was it really Adam? Was this some sort of treat for being a good employee for three years?

Oh, yeah. That made perfect sense. What man bought a woman thigh-highs and thong underwear if he wasn't after one thing—sex?

Sheila shook her head. He'd never shown her the slightest indication that he'd been interested in her in any way outside of her job. But tonight . . . if he wanted a good fuck she'd be happy to oblige. After all, wasn't that exactly what she'd fantasized about so many times?

That, and him actually loving her as much as she loved him.

No, I'm not going to allow myself to think that way. Not after years of wanting him in every way a woman could want a man.

She loved everything about him, from his powerful presence to the way he made each employee feel important. He didn't tolerate incompetence, but he had a gift for hiring well-qualified and efficient employees, and the company turnover had been practically nil. She also loved how generous he was with local charities, from breast cancer research to homeless shelters. She knew about his large donations only because all correspondence crossed her desk. Adam was a very private man, and she doubted anyone but she knew just how generous he was.

The doorbell rang, jolting Sheila from her thoughts, and it was all she could do not to hide in her closet just out of sheer nerves. She took a deep breath, picked up the evening bag and the long-stemmed rose, and walked to the living room. The air was cool on her bare shoulders, the satin dress rasped her nipples through the bra, and the thong snaked up her slit and pulled against her folds.

Greg had the door open and a man in a sleek Italian suit stood in the doorway, a strap of blue satin in his hands. The man was in his late thirties, she guessed, devastatingly handsome with sandy blond hair and ice blue eyes.

Behind him in the darkness Sheila saw a long black stretch limo at the curb, and her pulse picked up to an alarming pace. Her steps faltered as she felt a keen sense of disappointment. Was this blond man the one who had sent her the invitations?

Sheila raised her chin and walked across the room. When she stood directly in front of the tall, good-looking man holding the satin strip, he said, "Please turn around, Miss Lane. I've been instructed to blindfold you."

Chapter 3

Her jaw dropped. "Excuse me?"

Greg smirked, but the man's expression remained stoic. "Blindfold you. Now please turn around, if you will."

She glared at Greg. "Is this something you've done? Because if it is—"

"Not me, I swear." He held his hands up in surrender. "I'll check out the limo while you let robot-man blindfold you."

With a little shiver of uncertainty, and yet excitement, too, Sheila turned her back to the handsome hunk of a man. He carefully placed the blue satin over her eyes and tied it behind her head, just snug enough to keep it from slipping. In the distance she heard the sound of a door being opened and Greg's voice, but she couldn't understand a word he was saying.

While she strained to hear him, the man carefully turned her by the shoulders so that she was facing the same direction from which she heard Greg speaking.

"Let me guide you, Miss Lane." The man held her by her upper arm, helping her over the threshold and down the sidewalk toward the curb. Her heels clicked against the sidewalk, and the purr of the limo sounded louder now that her vision had been eliminated. Her steps were uncertain but the man strode confidently ahead, not giving her time to worry about tripping over her high heels and tumbling to the concrete.

The moment the man brought her to a stop, she felt her friend's hand on her wrist. Greg's lips brushed her forehead and she caught his familiar scent of testosterone, sunshine, and coconut suntan oil. "It's all right. Have fun, kiddo." And then he walked away.

Sheila took a deep but shaky breath and let the man help her into the limo.

Adam's gut tightened as he watched Greg Stuart kiss Sheila's forehead. Greg gave one more warning glance to Adam before turning away and sauntering back into the house.

In all honesty, Adam appreciated the fact that Sheila's friend had watched out for her, grilling him on what he intended to do with her. Adam had been polite, but restrained himself from telling Greg that he intended to fuck the hell out of Sheila Lane.

That, and win her heart.

He remained silent as the chauffeur helped Sheila into the limo and closed the door behind her, and he caught a whiff of her orange-blossom perfume. Adam studied her petite form as she settled into the seat, the long-stemmed rose and her evening bag clutched in her trembling hands. The dress had been made for her at the finest dress shop on Rodeo Drive. It presented her mouthwatering breasts to perfection and clung to every curve.

The color was perfect for her—it matched her sapphire eyes. Her hair was up in a softer, prettier style than she wore in the office, but he intended to set it free, to strip all of her bare.

Yes, Adam wanted more than Sheila Lane's body. He wanted her heart and soul. He intended to have all of her.

As soon as Dave Carson was in the driver's seat, Adam rapped his knuckles on the dividing glass, letting his chauffeur and friend know he was ready to leave.

"What—" Sheila started as soon as the limo went into motion, but Adam placed his hand over her lips, stifling her words.

"Shhhhhh," he murmured. "I want you to listen . . . and feel. All right?"

Sheila nodded, her lips rubbing against his palm. His cock ached at the feel of those lips and he wished only to push up her dress, pull aside the thong he knew she was wearing, and slide his cock deep within her.

But that would be soon enough. First he'd tease her, and bring her close to the brink again and again before he finally allowed her release, and before he allowed himself to have her. They had waited this long, and he wanted to make their first time more than memorable.

Sheila swallowed as she felt the limo move through traffic, and as she felt the heat of Adam's body near hers. Even without her sight, anywhere, anyplace, she could recognize the sound of his voice, his scent, his very presence.

But what was this all about?

He moved his hand from her mouth and placed it on her thigh. The warmth of his hand close to her center made her ache so badly it was all she could do not to squirm in her seat. "Mr. Tassoni?" she whispered. "What's going on?"

"No talking." Adam brushed his mouth over her ear and she

shivered. "After being in my employ all this time, Miss Lane, you know I expect my orders to be followed without question."

Sheila parted her lips to argue but he put his finger to them and murmured, "Quiet, my sweet." He pried the rose and evening bag from her tight grip. "I plan to pay you back for teasing me all these years, Sheila, even if it wasn't intentional. You are going to enjoy what I have in mind for both of us."

She made a sound of amazement and turned toward his voice, even though she couldn't see him. *Teasing* him?

"Oh, yes." He took her by the shoulders and moved her so that she was facing him as much as possible on the seat of the limo. Gently he brought her hands in front of her, lightly stroking her wrists before binding them with another piece of satin. "Did you think I never noticed the look in your eyes when you watched me? The way your tongue traced your lower lip when you brought files to me for my approval?"

Sheila made another sound, this time in protest, but he simply turned her so that now her back was to the luxurious leather seat, her hands bound in her lap. Her heart beat faster. He was dominating her like she'd always dreamed. She felt the limo make a turn. Where was he taking her?

"As much as I wanted you, there was nothing I could do about it as long as I was your employer." His hands cupped her breasts through the satin and a moan rose up in her. "Now I intend to have you, Miss Lane."

Confusion and amazement coursed through her veins at the thought of Adam wanting her sexually all this time, the same way she wanted him. She'd thought she'd been so careful to hide her longing for him, but apparently she'd made it only too obvious. "Adam," she whispered, but he placed one hand over her lips again.

"This is my time, sweetheart." He slid his hand from her mouth, down her throat, and settled at her cleavage.

Sheila whimpered and arched her back, offering herself to him. He could have her any way he wanted her, and the sooner the better. Her thong was so damp and her body was on fire.

She heard a soft intake of breath, and his thumbs circled her nipples through the satin of her dress. He brought the nubs to hard, tight peaks, making her squirm with desire.

In a slow and sensual movement, he pulled down the front of her strapless dress along with her bra, so that her breasts spilled out of their confines, into his hands, and she gasped. "Gorgeous," he murmured. "As lovely as I imagined, so many times." His warm breath fanned the soft skin of her breasts and her whole body was on fire. "Yes, payback will be very pleasurable."

She couldn't believe she was here. With Adam. And oh, lord, she wouldn't be able to take much more of his payback if this was any indication of how he intended to extract his payment. What an incredibly erotic feeling it was to be bound and blindfolded and totally at Adam's mercy, just like she'd fantasized about.

Adam pushed her breasts up high and Sheila moaned and squirmed as his tongue slowly circled one nipple. His tongue was hot and wet, and the light stubble on his face was rough against her delicate skin. Every movement, every touch had her body in flames. She felt the brush of his soft hair over her breasts, and then he turned to her other nipple, attending to it in the same manner.

She heard him draw a ragged breath as he pulled away. "Lie on your back, Sheila," he ordered at the same time he was turning her on the seat.

Her heart jumped. *Oh, my God. Was he going to take her now, like this?*

When she hesitated, he said, "Would you prefer I lower the glass and have my chauffeur watch while I enjoy your pleasures?"

The thought of being watched was somehow thrilling. Still she moved as quickly as she could, so that with his help she was on her back, her bound hands in front of her, her knees bent, and her dress up around her hips.

The limo purred along as it made its way through LA. Where, she didn't know, and right now she didn't care. All that mattered was the man who was pressing her thighs apart with his big hands, exposing her to the warm air and to his gaze.

He groaned and through her thong she felt the brush of his knuckles over her folds. "Already you're wet and swollen for me. And your scent . . . amazing."

Heat flushed through Sheila, a heady combination of embarrassment and arousal. She wished that she could see him, was allowed to speak to him, could touch him. Yet at the same time she enjoyed what he was doing to her and wanted everything he could give her.

Adam's cock ached, wanting so badly to slide into the little enchantress, and to fuck her until she screamed with her release. How easy it would be to take her now, and he knew she wanted him just as much.

He had been instantly attracted to Sheila, the moment he'd interviewed her for the administrative assistant position at Tassoni Investments. He had hired her for her extensive experience and her impeccable references. The fact that he wanted her never entered the equation. He had strict rules about employee fraternization, and that included himself.

She was an incredibly efficient assistant, firm and in control with clients and suppliers. When it came to her dealings with Adam she was equally professional, but Sheila tended to avoid his stare, lowering her gaze and stealing glances when she thought he wasn't looking.

He'd kept an eye on her, always wanting her. He hadn't been satisfied with any other woman since he'd known Sheila. He'd grown to appreciate her wit, her devotion to her friends, her smile.

She was made for him.

And now he had to feel her, had to taste her sweetness. With slow, deliberate movements he moved her thong out of the way with one hand and slipped a finger from his free hand into her hot center.

Sheila cried out and raised her hips toward him while he pounded his knuckles against her swollen folds and clit. The ache in his cock increased, but he concentrated on Sheila's pleasure. When her legs began trembling and he felt her close to climax, he withdrew from her soaked channel.

"No, my little tease. You may not come . . . yet." He slipped his finger into his mouth, tasting her juices and inhaling her scent. He closed his eyes as if savoring the finest of wines, the flavor, the bouquet. "You are delicious," he murmured, and brought his hand to her nose. "Smell your desire for me."

In the soft lighting of the limo he saw her cheeks flush. Her expression was one of pleasure and excitement, if not some uncertainty. Once again he sensed her desire to be dominated, to turn over control of her pleasure to him. She was giving herself willingly to him in every way, and he intended to fulfill her fantasies—to fulfill both of their fantasies.

"I have a couple of rules I'd like you to follow tonight." From a compartment in the limo he retrieved a highly sophisticated device that was about the size of a thin matchbook. It had a small clip on the back side, so fine that it could barely be seen. "Don't climax without my permission." He slipped the device inside her thong, against her clit, and clipped it to the damp material.

"Do you agree, Sheila, that if you don't hold back, you should be punished?" he asked as he reached into his pocket. "I promise you'll enjoy every minute of it."

Slowly she nodded, and her voice wavered. "Yes."

"Good." Adam smiled as his hand found the remote and pressed the "on" button.

Chapter 4

"A dam!" Sheila bucked her hips as her thong vibrated against her clit. Oh, God, she'd never be able to keep from coming. She was already so close to the edge, and he was driving her mad.

"Remember, Sheila." He lightly stroked the outside of one of her thighs with his fingers, adding to the sensations that wanted to explode within her. "Don't climax without my permission, or you'll get a taste of the little punishment I have in mind."

"Punishment," barely registered. She gave a strangled cry and clenched her legs together to keep from coming.

Adam placed his hands on the insides of her knees and pushed them back apart. "When we are alone, don't hide yourself from me. I want to see all of you."

Abruptly the vibrations stopped. Sheila sighed with relief, but at the same time almost cried from the need to come. Yes, she'd dreamed about him dominating her, but she hadn't known it would be such sweet torture.

"Very good." Adam slid his hands down her thighs and arranged her dress so that it covered her hips and garters, and she felt a little dizzy as he helped her up to a sitting position. He gently slipped her bra and the front of her dress back over her breasts.

Why wouldn't he let her come, damnit?

"Tonight you'll be mine, Sheila Lane." He lightly stroked her arm. "I'm in command of your pleasure, and I will have you."

Tonight, Sheila thought, *for tonight I'm his.* Just like she'd always wanted and dreamed.

One night of heaven—she'd take it.

"Adam," she whispered. "May I speak now?"

"Not yet." His warm breath caressed her face and then she felt his firm lips against the corner of her mouth. He grasped her face in his hands as he flicked his tongue over her bottom lip, then gently nipped at it. He bit her lip harder until she cried out. He plunged his tongue into her mouth, taking her deeply as he held her face tightly in his grip.

Sheila returned his kiss, hungry for him, for this man she had wanted for so long. She wished her hands were free so that she could touch him, could wind her arms around his neck and slide her fingers into his thick black hair. She loved the taste of him, the way he took her so fiercely and intensely, the feel of his light stubble chafing the soft skin around her mouth. God, how he took control was better than she had imagined. She could almost come just from the thought of what he had done already.

Adam withdrew from the kiss and she heard his breathing, more ragged now, as if he'd experienced the same incredible sensations she had.

"You taste perfect. Not only your mouth but your pussy, too." He gently freed her hands, slipping the satin away, and massaging her wrists where the cloth had been firmly tied. "Your skin is so soft. I can almost imagine how good it will feel to have your naked body beneath mine."

Was this real? It had to be a dream. Adam wanted her? She tingled from head to toe at the thought. She couldn't wait to feel his cock deep inside her. *Why hadn't he taken her already? Why was he driving her crazy like this?*

When he finally removed the blindfold, Sheila blinked, her vision coming back into focus. Her eyes met Adam's intense aquamarine gaze and more heat flooded her.

This was a dream. All of it. Everything that was happening made her feel like an erotic Cinderella.

Nick reached up and plucked the clip from her hair. Her heavy locks tumbled over her shoulders, caressing the bare skin. "I would love you to always wear your hair down." He fluffed it out with his fingers so that her hair curled over her breasts and back. "You are stunning."

His comment took her off guard. She'd never thought of herself as stunning, but coming from him she could almost picture it, as if seeing herself through his eyes. *Wow.*

"You can talk now." Fire still lit his gaze, but it was softer, warmer.

Sheila swallowed, not having any idea of what to say. She knew she must look like a besotted schoolgirl the way she was staring at him, and she struggled to find something to ask him. "Adam . . ." She gestured to the limo and then to her dress. "Why—why all of this?"

He gave her a sexy grin that made her want to melt into a puddle at his feet. "I have wanted you from the first day you began working for my company." He gently stroked a finger over her wrist, causing her to tremble. "Even though you were entirely professional, I could see the hunger in your eyes, the hunger that matched my own. I wanted to teach you not only the ropes of the business, but also the ways to pleasure me so that I could pleasure you in return."

His words seemed unreal, like she was really in some sort of fantasy. She shook her head, her hair sliding over her bare shoulders and the tops of her breasts. "But three years? Why did you wait so long? And why me?"

"What would you have wanted me to do?" Adam skimmed the back of his hand across her cheek, and she shivered. "Fire you so that I might fuck you?"

Heat rose again to Sheila's cheeks, and her folds ached even more at his words. She lowered her eyes, unable to meet his gaze.

"I needed time to get to know you, and you needed time to get to know me." Adam caught her chin in his hand and tipped her head up so that she was looking at him again. "I didn't want to take the chance of ruining the business relationship between us. It has become harder and harder to keep my hands off you. When the time came for me to sell my company, I knew it was the right time to take you, too."

Sheila wasn't exactly sure what he was saying, but she knew one thing and it absolutely amazed her. He wanted her sexually as badly as she wanted him, and he'd wanted her for just as long.

Tonight. He wanted her for tonight.

Right now she'd take him any way she could get him. It didn't matter that she loved him with everything she had. She needed a piece of him to cherish forever.

He gave her a sensual smile. "Will you be mine, and do everything I ask you to?"

Wild thoughts ran rampant through Sheila's mind. He was offering her all she had fantasized about, and more. How could she refuse? She took a deep breath and nodded. "Yes."

Brilliant colors from LA's city lights flashed by while the luxury automobile cruised the freeway. Her folds still ached and she knew she didn't want this night to stop.

He smiled as he handed her the evening bag from where it sat on the limo's wet bar. "You might want to freshen up a bit. I seem to have eaten off all of your lipstick."

Adam almost groaned out loud as Sheila worried her lower lip and dug into her sleek blue purse. That lower lip was still red from his bite, and he imagined sliding his cock into her mouth and deep into her throat.

Soon. Soon he'd have her in every way.

After he used the intercom to let Dave know he was ready to take Sheila to the nightclub, Adam lowered a lighted mirror built into his limo. He silently watched as Sheila touched up her makeup, from her eyes to her cheeks to her mouth. Her hands trembled as she applied it, and he wondered if it was from nerves or excitement, or both. As far as he was concerned she was beautiful without makeup, but he had a feeling she would feel more confident with it.

Especially since he was taking her out to claim her publicly. Later he would claim her privately.

Chapter 5

By the time Sheila had arranged her dress, hair, and makeup, the limo had arrived at an exclusive restaurant. Butterflies went berserk in her belly as Adam climbed out of the luxury vehicle, his movements as fluid and graceful as those of a panther.

He helped her out of the limo, then placed his hand at the small of her back as he escorted her to a famous restaurant and nightclub that Sheila had never dreamed she would ever go into.

"Mr. Tassoni," the concierge said as soon as they stepped into the establishment's foyer. "Right this way."

Sheila tried not to let her amazement show while they were led through a maze of tables alongside a dance floor. She felt completely out of place among so many famous people, from politicians and powerful businessmen to movie and television stars. Sequins and diamonds glittered all around her, and she caught whiffs of expensive perfume that wove through the delicious smells of the restaurant.

When they reached a corner table with an incredible view of the nighttime Los Angeles skyline, Adam assisted her, pushing in her chair before seating himself. The concierge handed each of them a menu, then bowed and left.

Adam sat close to her, surrounding her with his unique masculine scent and his powerful presence. She could hardly catch her breath. To take her mind off him, she took a moment to gaze at all that was around her from beneath her lashes, so that she didn't look like a starstruck kid.

The lighting was low and intimate, and at the center of the room was a dance floor. Beneath crystal chandeliers, couples danced to ballroom music performed by a live band. The music flowed over Sheila, and her years of training and love for dance made her want to be out on the floor with Adam.

When the waiter arrived, Adam ordered for them both and chose a fine chardonnay to go along with dinner. He poured each of them a glass of the wine, and handed Sheila her crystal stem.

"To tonight." He raised his glass and lightly clinked it against Sheila's, his aquamarine eyes focused on her as if she were the only person in the room. "An evening with a most delightful woman."

Warmth flooded Sheila at the intensity of his gaze and his words. Her throat was dry and she barely managed to respond, "To tonight."

Just as Sheila took a sip of her chardonnay, her thong vibrated against her clit. She almost spat her wine all over the fine linen tablecloth. "Adam," she whispered.

He slipped his arm around her and lightly stroked her collarbone with his thumb. "Yes?" he asked in a nonchalant tone as she clenched her thighs tight.

She could hardly speak because of the sensations coursing

through her body from the vibrator stimulating her clit. "I can't take much more."

Adam moved his mouth close to her ear. "You can."

"I'm too close to coming," she whispered in a hoarse voice.

His tone went deep. "Wait until I tell you to climax, my sweet Sheila."

Oh, lord. He was going to kill her.

Even when the waiter arrived with their appetizer, Adam left the vibrator on. Sheila avoided the waiter's gaze, afraid he would see how hard she was fighting to keep from coming.

To her relief, Adam turned off the vibrator long enough for her to draw back from the edge, at least for a few moments. However, throughout dinner he continued to turn it on, driving her to the precipice of an orgasm and back again. Sheila's clit was so sensitive that she was going out of her mind with the need to come.

He spent the evening touching her intimately, brushing his fingers along her arm and stroking her face. His eyes seemed to hint at more than simple lust, but Sheila refused to allow herself to think beyond the moment.

For dessert Adam ordered a single slice of a decadent chocolate cake, and insisted on feeding it to her. This time he didn't let up with the vibrator. In between bites of the dessert, when she'd managed to swallow the rich chocolate, she begged him to stop.

"I'm so close." She squirmed in her seat, but the movement only made her hotter. "Please, Adam."

He gave her an utterly wicked smile. "I'll have to punish you."

At the thought of being erotically punished by Adam, Sheila's skin flushed and her folds grew even more drenched. The vibrating thong kicked up a notch and it was too much. She bit her lip, hard, as an orgasm ripped through her unlike anything she'd ever experienced before. It started low in her abdomen and expanded outward, a hot flush of pleasure reaching every part of her being. Her body jerked in her seat and she kept her eyes lowered, praying no one could see her flushed face and her body shaking with her orgasm.

Adam caught her chin in his hand and raised her face so that his gaze met hers. "You're a very bad girl," he murmured as tremors continued to run rampant through her body. The way he said *bad girl* made her feel even more on fire.

"Please . . . turn it off." She tried to catch her breath, to speak without a quaver in her voice, but it was impossible. "I—I can't take anymore."

He gave her a smile, slipped his hand into his jacket pocket, and the vibrator stopped.

Sheila almost wept with relief. Her body tingled and throbbed, and she felt like everyone in the room must know she'd climaxed right there in the nightclub. The feeling of being watched only added to the aftershocks jarring her body.

"No one could tell." Adam dabbed a napkin at the corner of her mouth and brushed the back of his hand over her breast as he moved away. "Only I know how badly you've misbehaved."

By the deep, intense tone of his voice she knew he intended to deal out her punishment soon, and that she would enjoy every minute of it.

When they had finished the dessert and Adam had paid the bill, he pulled out Sheila's chair and helped her to stand. Her legs trembled and she prayed she'd be able to walk.

With his hand on her elbow, Adam escorted Sheila along the edge of the dance floor and then away from the crowd, the talking, and the laughter. He led her down a long and richly paneled hallway lit by occasional brass sconces that gave off a soft golden glow. It became so quiet that she heard only the sound of their footsteps on thick carpeting and the pounding of her heart.

They finally reached a door where a man in an impeccably starched suit stood with his hands behind his back. "May I assist you, Mr. Tassoni?"

"Is this room available?" When the man gave an affirmative nod, Adam slipped out his money clip and handed the man a couple of hundred-dollar bills. "See to it that we're not disturbed."

"Yes, sir." The man gave a quick nod and the money vanished within his suit jacket. He immediately returned to his former position, hands behind his back and his expression stoic.

Sheila's cheeks burned as Adam led them into a luxurious men's bathroom. Without a sound, the heavy mahogany door closed behind them. The walls of the front sitting room were dark paneled and an opening in one wall led from the plush room to where Sheila presumed the toilets were.

The sitting room carpet was a thick, rich forest green, and the countertops and sinks were obviously of extremely expensive marble. Fine linen hand cloths were stacked beside the sinks, and the room smelled faintly of cigar smoke and almond-scented soap.

"What's that man going to think?" she whispered, as if the attendant might hear.

Adam led her to a marble countertop before a huge mirror illuminated by low, seductive lighting. "He probably thinks I'm going to fuck you."

She went even hotter all over at the thought of the man knowing what they were doing—if in fact Adam intended to take her right then and there.

"Face the mirror and brace your hands on the countertop," he ordered in a low, rumbling voice. "Now bend over and widen your thighs."

Sheila found herself following his directions automatically. After she set her evening bag on the countertop she bent over and waited, her body trembling with nerves. "What are you going to do?"

"Mmmmm . . ." He pressed his hips against her backside, and through his slacks she felt his hard cock along the cleft of her ass. She watched his reflection in the mirror while he reached around and lowered the bodice of her dress and her strapless bra so that her breasts were bared. She shivered with excitement, longing, need, and even a little fear of whatever punishment he had in mind.

Her body throbbed as she watched him knead her nipples and felt his rough, masculine hands against her soft nubs. "I've wanted to touch your breasts for so long." His voice was hoarse as he cupped them in his palms. "You will definitely need another little punishment."

She swallowed her fear and excitement as he leaned back and pushed her dress up over her hips so that her backside was bared to him. All she was wearing were the thong, garters, and thigh-high stockings he'd bought for her. She could just imagine how she must look to him.

"Damn but I love your ass." He rubbed her butt cheeks with his palm and she moaned aloud. "Do you know why you're being punished?"

"For climaxing when you told me not to." Sheila's voice trembled as her eyes met his in the mirror. What else had he said? Oh, yeah. "And for—for teasing you."

"That's right, my sweet." He raised his hand and swatted her. *Hard.*

Sheila yelped at the sudden pain. To her surprise the tingling melted into a feeling that made her wetter for him. It actually felt kind of good. But when he swatted her again, the pain was sharper this time. It hurt, but then she was filled with pleasure that made her ache.

"Watch me spank you in the mirror." Adam swatted her again, the smack loud in the quiet room. "See how enchanting you are?" he added, his Italian accent even stronger.

Her eyes widened as she watched their reflections. He was so handsome, so big and powerful, and by the gleam in his eyes she knew he was enjoying this erotic punishment. When she turned her gaze to herself, she couldn't believe how seductive she looked with her breasts naked, her dress up over her ass, her eyes wide, and her lips parted.

Again and again he spanked her, and she tensed before every swat as she watched his hand sweep down to land on her ass.

Her breasts swung with every slap of his hand and her nipples ached. Her sex was on fire, her folds swollen and her clit throbbing. "Please may I come?" she asked as he landed another slap on her ass.

"No." He spanked her again. "You'll have to wait until I tell you it's all right, sweetheart." Another swat. "My flogger would make your ass an even prettier shade of pink."

She groaned, her ass burning and tingling. When he finally stopped, she breathed a sigh of relief. Much more and she would have come even if it meant another punishment. Then it hit her. "Flogger?" she said.

"Stand and face me." He pulled down her dress over her stinging ass and she turned. "Imagine soft suede straps swatting you instead of my hand. Would you like that?"

He was so handsome she could hardly take her eyes off his face. That devilish gleam in his eyes added to his incredibly sexy appeal. She knew he wouldn't do anything to *really* hurt her and if it meant spending more time with him she'd take that flogger.

"Yes." She sucked in a deep breath. "For you."

He smiled and reached into his pocket and pulled out a fine strand of diamonds that sparkled in the room's low lighting. Before she realized what he was doing, he looped one end of the chain over one of her nipples and tightened it, then did the same with the other end. She gasped at the intense feeling, again of pain mixed with pleasure, as her nipples engorged with blood.

"This nipple chain signifies you are mine," he murmured as he gently tugged at it. "Will you wear it?"

His . . . it meant she was his . . . at least for tonight. "Yes," she whispered. *God yes.*

"Good." He smiled and pushed down on her head, gently forcing her to her knees in front of his obvious erection. "Now for your second punishment."

Chapter 6

Sheila's knees sank into the plush carpeting and her skin prickled with excitement, knowing what he would want now.

"Unfasten my slacks." Adam kept his hands clenched in her hair. "I want your hot, wet mouth on me now, like I've imagined countless times."

She still had a hard time believing he'd wanted her so much.

She bit her lip as she undid his trousers and unzipped his fly, her hands trembling and fumbling with the fastenings. She pulled down his boxers, and his thick, long, luscious cock slipped out right before her lips.

"That's it, sweetheart." He gently pushed her head closer to him. "Take me in your mouth, my little tease."

She slipped his cock through her lips and sighed at the feel of his hard length sliding to the back of her throat. She swirled her tongue over the ridges and contours, and reveled in his distinctly male scent and the tight curls at the base of his cock.

"Play with your nipples while you suck me." His tone was powerful and commanding as he kept his grip on her hair and thrust his hips toward her face.

Sheila brought her hands to her nipples and caressed the incredibly hard nubs and the rings that were taut around them. The diamond chain swung between her breasts, lightly bouncing against her soft skin. The ache in her increased so much that she thought she'd come just from the feel of his cock in her mouth and her own hands on her breasts.

"You're so damn good." Adam thrust his hips a little harder. "You look even more beautiful than ever."

His declaration made her hotter and more excited. She squirmed, wanting to climax but knowing she'd receive another punishment if she did. This was her second punishment, being unable to come while she pleasured him and herself.

And it was such incredibly sweet torture that she could hardly stand it.

"I'm about to come." His voice was hoarse and she could tell he was close as his cock grew harder and his balls drew up. "You'd better let me know if you'd rather have me come all over your breasts or in your mouth."

In response, Sheila sucked him harder. Adam groaned out loud and his hips bucked against her face as his warm fluid spurted down her throat. Sheila drank from him as he continued to pump in and out of her lips until he finally said, "Stop," and pulled her head away from him.

Sheila remained on her knees looking up at Adam as he tucked his still thick, moist cock into his boxers, then zipped up his trousers. The entire time he kept his gaze on her, an intense look in his aquamarine eyes.

She fought to keep from squirming with her need to come. "Please may I climax now?"

"No." He extended his hand and helped her to rise so that she was standing before him. "You'll have to wait," he added with a smile that told her he had much more erotic pleasures in store for her.

Adam palmed her large breasts and raised them at the same time that he lowered his head. Sheila moaned and grabbed his shoulders as he sucked and licked one nipple, then paid the same attention to the other. "You are such a lovely woman," he murmured as he paused. "Inside and out."

The chain swung between her breasts and he lightly tugged on it with one finger as he sucked her nipples. The need to climax was so intense that tears pricked the backs of Sheila's eyes. She wanted to beg and plead, but she knew it wouldn't do any good. Finally he raised his head and arranged her bra over the nipple chain, then the front of her dress.

The corner of his mouth curved into a roguish grin. "You might want to freshen up your lipstick again. I seem to be wearing it on my cock."

Heat rushed to Sheila's face, but it was more a feeling of excitement than any sense of embarrassment. She touched up her makeup and her lipstick while Adam stood behind her and fluffed her hair over her shoulders. Her nipples were still swollen from the nipple chain, and she could see they were obviously hard through the bra and the satin of her dress.

Adam watched her like he couldn't take his eyes off her. "You are gorgeous in that color," he murmured. "Hell, you're gorgeous in anything you wear." His smile was sinful as he turned her around in his arms. "But I'll bet you're even sexier in nothing at all."

Sheila's cheeks had never burned so much in her life as they had tonight. He led her out of the men's facilities and thank God the corridor was empty, save for the attendant.

The attendant simply nodded and said, "Good evening, Mr. Tassoni."

"Do you do this a lot?" she said as soon as they were out of hearing range.

Adam slapped her on the ass and she barely contained a yelp of surprise as her gaze shot to him. "I think you need another punishment." A hint of amusement lit his eyes.

While Adam led Sheila to the dance floor, he couldn't believe how hard he was for her again. When she'd slipped her mouth over his cock, it had taken all his power not to come at once. She'd looked so enticing, his diamond chain sparkling between her breasts while she rolled her nipples between her thumbs and forefingers.

And hell, her mouth had been so hot and sweet it had driven him insane with need. Just seeing her looking up at him with those incredible sapphire eyes while he fucked her mouth nearly sent him over the edge the moment she ran her tongue along his cock.

A slow song was playing when he guided her onto the dance floor and brought her into his arms. She put her hands on his shoulders and he placed his at her waist, drawing her close so that his erection pressed against her belly. She felt so good in his embrace, her warm, soft body against his.

Sheila was petite, her head just reaching his chest, and Adam had to lean down to nuzzle the top of her head. He breathed in her soft, sweet perfume, a mixture of orange blossoms and her own unique womanly scent. He lightly rubbed his thumbs along her waist, enjoying the feel of her curves beneath his hands.

Despite the fact that he knew most of the people there, Adam ignored everyone around them and focused on the incredible woman in his arms. He loved the way she snuggled against him, her full breasts pressed against his abs. He could feel the nipple chain through the satin of her dress, and it made his cock harder to know she was wearing his token of ownership.

He had staked his claim. She was his and he would spend the night showing her he wasn't going to ever let her go.

But in truth *she* owned *him*, heart and soul.

"You're the loveliest woman here," he murmured into her hair.

Sheila gave a sigh of contentment as they moved to the slow beat. "And you say the sexiest things."

He slipped one hand from her waist into his jacket pocket and turned on the vibrator. Sheila's gaze shot up to his immediately, her cheeks turning pink and her body stiffening in his arms.

"Adam." She bit her lower lip and squirmed against him, pressing hard against his cock. "God, I can't take much more of this."

"You will." He kissed her hair and smiled. He loved that the device was vibrating against her clit, making her wetter for him. He only wished he could put his mouth there instead, to lick her folds and taste her thoroughly. "I'll have to punish you again if you come."

Sheila moaned against him and dug her fingers into the jacket covering his shoulders. "I'm so close, Adam," she whispered. "I'm about to come."

In response he lowered his head and captured her mouth with his. Her body trembled and she moaned as he bit her lower lip. And when he thrust his tongue into her warmth she gave a little cry into his mouth and her body shuddered against his. He could feel the waves of her orgasm as he kissed her long and deep.

"Stop," she begged when he pulled away from the kiss, her

body still trembling with aftershocks, one miniorgasm after another. "Please. It's too much."

Adam gave her a mock reproving look as he reached into his pocket. "Now you've earned another punishment, you bad girl."

He shut off the device and she went limp against him and gave a little groan. "You don't play fair, Adamo Tassoni."

Adam leaned back so that he could see her flushed face and her eyes, which had that just-got-fucked look. Only he hadn't fucked her—yet.

"Let's go," he said, feeling the incredible need to get her alone, *now*. "I've got to have you."

Chapter 7

The urgency in Adam's voice thrilled Sheila to her core. The way he said *"I've got to have you,"* made tingles zip from her belly to her folds.

If only he wanted *her* and not just sex.

But she wasn't going to think past tonight.

Adam whipped out his cell phone and called his chauffeur to bring the limo around, and the next thing she knew they were slipping out of the nightclub to where the limo waited.

The driver already stood at the passenger door, waiting to let them into the luxurious vehicle. As she slipped into its plush confines, Adam paused a moment to give the driver instructions, but too quietly for Sheila to hear.

Sheila's pulse raced and her heart hammered as Adam slid into the limo and the chauffeur closed the door behind them. The minute they were alone he took her face in his palms and kissed her with so much urgency and need that it robbed her of her breath. Lord, that man could kiss. He nipped at her lower lip, drawing her mouth wide and open for him, and then he plunged his tongue deep inside.

When he finally broke off the kiss they were both breathing hard, and she was barely conscious of the limo moving through Los Angeles traffic and the glitter of the lights zipping by.

"Damn but you drive me crazy, woman," he said in a voice rough with passion.

She drove *him* crazy? "Don't you think you've gotten enough payback, Adam?" she said, half teasing and half serious. "*You've* been driving me nuts all night."

"Hmmm . . ." He gave her a thoughtful look. "I think you have a punishment or two still coming."

At the word *punishment*, a shiver ran through Sheila. Her butt still tingled from the earlier spanking, her pussy throbbed from the orgasm on the dance floor, and her nipples ached from the diamond chain.

How much more could she take?

He reached into a hidden compartment and drew out a black leather handle with long suede strips attached to it.

The flogger.

Her gaze shot to Adam's face.

He took the object and gently caressed her cheek with the soft suede. "Do you still want to feel this on your ass, knowing it's me controlling your pain and pleasure?"

Sheila couldn't speak, because now he was trailing the flogger over her breasts in a slow, sensual caress. With his free hand he tugged down the front of her dress and her bra, freeing her full breasts. The diamond chain glittered in the limo's low lighting and her nipples were dark purple and achingly hard.

"Yes," she finally said. "I want *everything*."

"Good. Now take off your dress and bra." He slid the flogger down to where the satin material of her dress was now bunched. "Leave on the garters, thong, and the heels."

The words and act made it seem suddenly forbidden and exciting, as if he were still her employer and taking her the way she'd always dreamed. How many times had she fantasized about a moment like this? Hundreds of times, at least. It had been three years worth of fantasizing.

This was far better than fantasy. Far better than being alone with her vibrator.

City lights shimmered outside the darkened windows as the car ran smoothly through the streets. Adam pressed a button on a panel and a soft, seductive melody filled the back of the limo.

While she undressed, she couldn't help but think about the chauffeur and the fact that he must know what was going on in the back, much like the attendant at the men's facilities. Somehow the knowledge made her feel much naughtier. It thrilled her, in fact.

Adam watched as Sheila shimmied out of her dress, his cock hard and aching. Her breasts swayed as she worked the satin over her hips. She let the dress slide to the floor of the limo, and he almost groaned out loud at the sight of her clad in the blue garters and thigh-highs he'd picked out for her.

Before he lost control and took her right then, Adam grabbed her by the waist. She let out a little yelp as he flung her across his lap, her ass sticking up and her upper half hanging upside down.

"What are you doing?" she said in a muffled voice. "Um, Adam?"

He lazily trailed the flogger over her ass cheeks and felt her tremble. "It's time for a little more punishment."

Sheila swallowed, remembering all too well the orgasm on the dance floor. She felt dizzy from the rush of blood to her head as she hung upside down over his lap, his erect cock pressed into her belly. And she felt dizzy from excitement, too. What would it feel like to be flogged by Adam. Her former *boss*.

He slapped her with the flogger's straps, so lightly that it felt like a mere caress. "I need to teach you a lesson, Sheila."

This time he brought the flogger down a little harder and she gave a cry of surprise. The next swat and the next were harder yet, but the bit of pain turned immediately into tingling pleasure. It stung a little, then it felt good, like the spanking he'd given her earlier.

Abruptly Adam stopped, needing to taste his woman. He easily picked her up and laid her on her back on the limo seat, her hair splayed behind her and her thighs pressed far apart. The damn thong was getting in his way. He reached into another compartment and drew out a small knife.

"Hold still," he ordered, and Sheila's eyes grew wide as he brought the knife close to her. In a couple of quick movements he'd cut the thong and flung it to the side, along with the tiny vibrator. He tossed the knife into the compartment and immediately turned his attention back to Sheila.

He slid his palms under her ass and brought her up, and buried his mouth against her pussy. She cried out and squirmed as if fighting another orgasm. "Adam!"

He raised his head and gave her a warning look. "Don't come, sweetheart. If you do it's going to be a long wait until I fuck you."

Sheila almost wept with need. Her ass still tingled, and his mouth against her was driving her wild. But she needed his cock inside her. She could wait, she could hold back. She gritted her teeth and clenched her hands into the fine leather upholstery, fighting off her orgasm with everything she had.

Just as she thought she couldn't take any more, Adam stopped.

He was so large and powerful that in an easy movement he brought her into his lap so that she was straddling him in the center of the limo. The feel of his slacks between her bare thighs was wild and erotic. He was fully clothed and she was mostly naked, one of her favorite fantasies. It was like the man could read her mind.

"You've been a good girl by behaving in the limo, and you deserve a reward." He unbuttoned his slacks and released his cock from his boxers. "Now I'm going to fuck you."

Yes!

Sheila placed her hands on his shoulders and rose up, ready to take him after he sheathed himself with a condom. The limo purred along, city lights glittering like gems, yet she hardly saw them. She was so ready to be taken by Adam.

When he placed the head of his cock at her core, he only slid in a fraction before lifting her up again. She groaned, wanting him to drive into her with everything he had. Instead he held her completely still, his cock barely an inch inside her as he licked and sucked her nipples.

With a moan of frustration, she tilted her head forward, her long hair brushing her naked shoulders and forming a curtain around them.

"What do you want, Sheila?" he asked as he paused and looked up at her.

Her eyes focused on his and she had no problem telling him exactly what she wanted. "I want you inside me."

"Do you want me to fuck you?" He lowered her a little farther down on his cock. "Is that what you want?"

God that was hot, the way he said the word.

Sheila nodded. "Yes. *Please* fuck me!"

He gripped her hips and brought her down hard, driving his full length deep inside her.

She cried out at the surprise of his fullness, the feel of finally having his cock in her core. He kept a tight grasp on her hips, and raised her up and down along his length while his mouth ravaged each of her engorged nipples. An orgasm began rising and rising within her, almost too strong to fight.

"Don't come," he said in between suckling her breasts. "Wait until I tell you."

It felt so damn good to be inside his woman after all this time. Adam couldn't get enough of her and he had to fight to hold back. But he forced himself to maintain control as he fucked her, drawing their mutual pleasure out as long as possible.

Slowly he slid her up and down his cock, watching her face. She was covered with a light sheen of sweat and she was biting her lower lip. Gradually he increased their pace, pounding harder and harder into her, causing her to cry out with every thrust of his cock.

When he finally couldn't wait any longer, he shouted, "Now, Sheila!"

She screamed as her body jerked and quaked against his. His own orgasm roared through him. Heat burned him and he felt like he was on fire. A fucking inferno was blazing within him.

When neither could take any more Sheila collapsed against him, her breathing hard and fast, matching his own.

"Miss Lane," he murmured as he tried to catch his breath, "you have most excellent qualifications."

Sheila rose up and gave him a sated smile. "Mr. Tassoni, you certainly have great benefits."

Chapter 8

Monday morning Sheila sat at her desk, unable to concentrate on her work. She stared out the window, reliving Friday night, remembering every last detail of her time with Adam.

Thrills continually rippled through her belly and her breasts at the thought of their night, and how many times he'd taken her in the back of the limo. She swore she could still smell his scent on her skin, enjoy the feel of his hands on her body.

He'd dropped her off at her condo at two in the morning, and had given her an earth-shattering kiss at her doorstep. That kiss had been deep and possessive, and she'd hoped that he would call her over the weekend.

But he hadn't.

While the low hum of voices hovered in the background, Sheila sighed and watched clouds drift lazily by. She was wearing Adam's diamond chain and she felt her tight nipples beneath her jacket. The chain kept her in a state of constant arousal, and she wondered again why she had worn it to work.

Of course she knew why. The chain was a part of her wonderful night with Adam, his gift to her. It was part of the memories she would treasure for a lifetime.

Likely he had just been satisfying a sexual urge, and now he would leave her wanting him. Would she ever meet any man who'll live up to Adamo Tassoni?

The answer came easily to her. "No," she whispered.

She slipped out of her chair and walked to Adam's former office. Sometime today the movers would bring in Edward Johnson's belongings, but for now she swore she could still feel Adam's presence, could smell his masculine scent.

Sheila leaned against the door frame of his office and crossed her arms beneath her breasts, hugging herself tight. His huge mahogany desk and shelves were bare, his expensive decor gone. All she had left were memories, but Lord, what memories she had now.

"You really should stop embarrassing yourself like this." Kate Baron's haughty voice came from behind her.

Straightening to her full height—which was about five inches shorter than Kate—Sheila turned to face the bitch. "Don't you have throats to slit or something?"

Kate narrowed her eyes. "You're just a little nothing. Now that your lord and master is gone, I can get your ass fired."

Sheila opened her mouth to tell Kate exactly where she could shove her threat when she felt a familiar presence. Hands gripped her shoulders, forcing her to turn around. Before she realized what was happening, she was facing Adam. He looked both angry and possessive all at once. He cupped the back of her head and brought her mouth roughly to his. He gave her such a soulsearing kiss that her whole body went weak and she melted against him. She felt him pull the clip from her hair and it all tumbled down around her shoulders in a mass while he worked his fingers through it.

When he drew back, his expression was intense, as if he was telling her a thousand things with that one look. "Good morning, sweetheart," he murmured. "I'm sorry I couldn't call you this weekend. I had a family emergency."

He draped a possessive arm around her shoulders and turned to Kate. "You will never speak to my future wife in such a manner again, Ms. Baron."

What? Sheila's head started buzzing with what Adam had just said. *My future wife. My future wife*, kept going through her mind. She stared up at him, feeling as if her head was going to float away because of the surreal moment.

Kate raised her chin, incredulity in her eyes. With her whole posture rigid, she turned and walked away.

Adam turned his attention to the speechless Sheila. The next thing she knew he eased down onto one knee and looked up at her. From his pocket he withdrew a black velvet box and snapped it open. Inside was a sparkling marquise diamond—at least 2 carats—surrounded by sapphires. He took her hand in his and her head spun, unable to believe what was happening.

"That's crazy." Speaking and breathing didn't come easy to her. "We hardly know each other."

"Okay, so maybe I jumped ahead of myself but it was worth it to see the look on her face." He gave an almost boyish smile. "But, sweetheart, I did fall in love with you long ago." His aquamarine eyes sparked with fire. "And now it's time to make you mine, for good."

"Wow." She swayed a little as her entire body buzzed. "I've loved you forever, Adam." She gave him a sudden smile as incredible joy filled her. "And now you're mine for keeps."

Adam gave her that soul-melting smile she loved and he slid the ring on her finger.

He rose up, towering over her, and cupped her face in his palms. His mouth met hers, this time gentle and sweet. A long, deep kiss that made her heart pound and her knees weak. She clung to the lapels of his suit, barely able to stand on her own.

When he finally drew back, she could only stare up at him in wonder and love. But then sudden applause broke out around them, and Sheila flushed when she saw virtually the entire staff of Tassoni Investments smiling and applauding, including her friend Andi and Edward Johnson. The only one not smiling was Kate Baron, who was still looking shell-shocked.

In one smooth, powerful movement, Adam scooped up Sheila in his arms, and she gave a little cry of surprise and clung to his neck. Edward approached and said, "Looks like I just lost my office assistant."

Adam grinned and looked down at Sheila. "Looks like I just gained a wife."

They rode in the limo to his home in Beverly Hills, and Adam couldn't keep his hands off Sheila. He kissed her, touched her, held her tight. It was all he could do not to strip her bare and take her right in the limo. Again and again.

When they arrived at his mansion, Adam carried his future bride through the enormous home and upstairs to the master bedchamber. He carefully set her on her feet beside the bed. Her eyes were wide, her blond hair was tousled, and her mouth was red from his kisses.

"I can't believe this is happening." Sheila's throat worked and she laid her small hand on his chest. "I had no idea you felt the same way I do. Friday night . . . I thought you just wanted sex."

"How could you not know?" He brushed the back of his hand over her cheek. "Didn't you notice how often I made it a point to call you into my office to go over files that I could have reviewed alone? Or the times I leaned over your shoulder while you worked and breathed in the scent of you? It was torture having you near, but it didn't matter. I *had* to be close to you."

Sheila shivered as Adam slid her jacket from her shoulders and let it drop to the floor. He smiled when he saw how taut her nipples were through the fine fabric of her blouse, and the rough outline of the diamond chain.

"You wore it," he said, his tone one of pleasure and surprise as he unbuttoned her blouse and reached for the nipple chain. He lightly tugged on it and she gasped at the exquisite sensation.

She caught her breath as his knuckles brushed along her skin and hovered at the pretty, lacy pink bra she'd bought that weekend at a lingerie shop, along with matching panties. She hadn't known if she would ever be with Adam again, but she'd felt so risqué just wearing the lingerie beneath her clothing with the hope that he would see them.

And here she was, in his bedroom, after he'd proposed to her.

She was going to be Adam's wife.

Slowly he undressed her as if cherishing every curve of her body. When she stood naked before him she burned even hotter for him.

He kicked off his shoes, then let her undress him. He couldn't take his eyes off his woman as she pushed his jacket from his shoulders and to the floor, then unbuttoned his shirt and discarded it just as easily. But when her hands reached his waistband, she trailed her fingers over the taut outline of his cock, looking up at him with a mischievous expression.

"You'd better hurry, sweetheart." His aquamarine eyes burned with desire. "I'm about to take you just as I am."

Sheila smiled and unfastened his trousers, enjoying the power she had over him.

When they were both naked, Adam carried her to the bed, his body hot against hers. He gently set her on the burgundy satin comforter and eased onto the bed beside her so that they were facing each other, his hard cock pressed against her belly and her nipples brushing his chest.

"You have no idea how long I've dreamed of this," he murmured as he lightly skimmed his fingers along her curves.

"I think I might." Sheila raised her hand to trace his lower lip with her thumb. "You have been the subject of every fantasy I've had since I met you."

"It killed me knowing I had to wait for the right time." With a self-deprecating smile he shook his head. "So many times I wanted to break the rules, to say to hell with it and bend you over my desk and fuck you. To mark you as mine."

Tingles skittered through Sheila's belly and she gave him a little grin. "That was one of my favorite fantasies. The spanking part, too. I loved that Friday night."

He rolled her onto her back and slid between her thighs. "I have a feeling you're going to be naughty and need lots of spankings."

She gave him a wicked grin. "I can be a very, very bad girl."

"Don't I know it." Adam dipped his head and flicked his tongue over her nipple. "But now I intend to make love to you."

A moan escaped Sheila's lips and she arched her breasts higher, wanting more from him. He seemed to read her mind, latching onto one nipple and sucking it and the loop that kept her nipple swollen and hard.

"You taste so damn good," he murmured as he began easing down her body, lightly lapping at her skin and erotically tormenting her.

When he reached her folds he slid two fingers inside her, working them in and out as he licked and sucked her clit. Just as her body began to tremble with an oncoming orgasm, Adam rose up and placed his cock at her center. For a long moment his gaze met hers and she read his love as clearly as she felt her own.

He slid into her with one slow thrust and stopped, his arms braced to either side of her shoulders. Sheila whimpered at the feel of him and she squirmed, wanting him to take her. But he kept his intense gaze on her, his powerful body still between her thighs.

"You're mine," he said, his voice filled with possession and power as he slowly began thrusting in and out of her. "All mine. Say it, Sheila."

"Yes." She could barely speak as she lightly scraped her fingernails over his back. "I'm yours, Adam. Forever."

He gave her a look of extreme satisfaction and began moving in and out of her, harder and faster. Sheila met his every thrust, her passion building and building until she shook with the effort not to come.

"Now," she said, "come with me now, Adam."

He shuddered and cried out, "Sheila!" and she felt his hot fluid pumping inside her channel.

Her own orgasm soared through her, a maelstrom of sensation intensified by knowing that Adam returned her love. His hard body was pressed tightly to hers, but her orgasm seemed as though it might never stop—as if it might rip her apart. Her core clenched and unclenched around his cock and waves of feeling kept coursing through her body.

Adam rolled onto his side and brought her with him so that they were face-to-face, her leg over his hip so that his cock was still inside her. Gradually their breathing slowed and the corner of his mouth turned up in a sexy smile. Sweat dripped from his hair and she smelled the scent of their sex. Nothing had ever smelled so good, and no one had ever looked so wonderful as Adam did at that very moment.

"You're hired, Miss Lane," he said in a teasing tone.

Sheila laughed. "I accept the position, Mr. Tassoni."

Wicked Surrender

Chapter 1

She could do this. She could be a submissive for one weekend. Now she just needed to find the right Dom to rock her world.

In the shadows near the resort bar, Andi Kelly clutched her martini glass so tightly she was afraid the slender stem would snap. The Cosmopolitan would hopefully begin its magic soon, allowing her to relax, at least a little.

How many times had she fantasized about having a BDSM relationship, if only in the bedroom? From the time she read that book about a ball-busting bitch of a lawyer who secretly wanted to be dominated and went for it, Andi had thought of what it would be like to be in that woman's place—the thought of giving up control and allowing a man to arouse her sexually and spank and flog her. It was an intriguing and exciting thought that made her sex ache.

She let her gaze rove the room as she took another sip of her Cosmo, still trying to relax. It was one thing to fantasize about something, another to go through with it.

Maybe it was a strange fantasy. Maybe she was crazy. But she *wanted* this. She needed this. Being one of the three Vice Presidents of an investment firm meant she had to be in total control at all times. In control of her emotions and whatever situation she was in. She couldn't show weakness because in the high-powered business world, any sign of weakness could destroy you and your reputation.

No, it wasn't such a strange fantasy after all. It was a way of releasing everything and not having to worry about anything. Giving up control. It probably wouldn't be easy, but she wanted this.

What a way to have great sex, too, without worrying about a relationship. She had a career to think about, and wasn't ready to commit to any kind of ties. Some men she'd met had wanted relationships—more than she'd been willing to give. That or they'd just wanted to fuck around and use her, and she wasn't about to put up with that crap. So she'd gotten away from dating, and it had been way too long since she'd been laid.

This retreat was all about sex and domination, mixed with a little pain and a lot of pleasure. No strings, no attachments, and she'd be able to choose her Dom. Hopefully she'd find one she'd love to have mind-bending sex with.

Her gaze took in the room, filled with seemingly normal everyday people—they could be lawyers, doctors, secretaries, construction workers, computer programmers, waitresses—just ordinary people with one thing in common. . . .

They were all into kink—BDSM.

Andi took a bigger gulp of her Cosmo, and the heat of the alcohol burned down her throat, landing in her empty stomach. Oh, she'd be feeling the buzz soon, all right. A little confidence courtesy of Stoli.

The resort's dimly lit lounge smelled of cigarette smoke, beer, and wine, along with the tantalizing aroma of the appetizers displayed on a table along one wall of the room. Hot wings, spinach dip, cheese and crackers . . . Andi's stomach growled and she hugged herself with one arm while she took another sip of her Cosmo. She was hungry, but she wasn't sure she wanted to eat—she might throw up, as nervous as she was. Instead she closed her eyes for a moment and listened to the throb of the music, an alternative rock song that pounded in time with her pulse.

When Andi had told her friend Sheila Tassoni about her fantasy to be a submissive for a night, maybe even a few nights, Sheila had surprised—no, shocked—her by recommending a weekend away at a country club resort . . . but to its patrons it was known as the Bondage Club. Andi had asked Sheila how she knew about the Club, but her friend had just blushed and shrugged. Apparently Sheila and her new husband, the former owner of Tassoni Investments, were into kink themselves.

Interesting.

Andi and Sheila had met at the annual Christmas party when Sheila first started as Adam Tassoni's secretary. Andi had hit it off with Sheila from the first moment they'd started talking at the party. Andi liked Sheila's honesty, frankness, and modesty. They'd started going out to coffee shops and talking over frappuccinos about anything and everything. Sheila had confided in Andi about how much she had fallen for her boss, who didn't even notice her. Turned out he had, he just couldn't do anything about it until he sold the company.

She smiled. It was a little like Cinderella and Prince Charming. Once Adam Tassoni was free of the restrictions that had kept him from crossing the line from boss to lover to husband, he had claimed Sheila at once.

Andi opened her eyes, took a deep breath, and glanced at the bartender before turning her gaze back to the room. So far she had escaped notice—or maybe her body language had been read loud and clear. *Don't come near me. I'm scared half out of my mind.*

Which wasn't like Andi at all. Because of her tenacity, her ability to close the deal like no one else could, she had been promoted to Vice President of Tassoni Investments sometime ago. Known as a tough but fair boss, she could run circles around any man when it came to her work. Any man but Derrick Macintyre, that is.

Where Adam Tassoni hadn't been able to cross the line between boss and secretary, Andi hadn't felt the same line was there between employees. Maybe she was just fooling herself in that regard. But if she would have a chance to fuck anyone at Tassoni Investments, it would be her fellow VP, Derrick Macintyre.

A delicious shiver ran down her spine as her imagination took over and she pictured Derrick's big, hard body between her thighs.

But then she frowned at the thought of the ruthless investor. He was her equal at the investment firm, also a VP, but he had such a dominating presence. It irritated her—yet at the same time both his ruthlessness and his dominating bearing turned her on. Something about him always made her have to fight to keep from squirming in her chair at board meetings. Just looking at him made her nipples taut and her panties damp. The fact that he was one of the sexiest men alive might have something to do with that.

When she and Derrick had been alone going over a file, she had felt like the air around them snapped with electricity. And the way their eyes met, or the brush of their fingers—how could he not feel something, too?

Jeez. What the hell was the matter with her? She'd given Sheila the advice to "go for it" with Adam, and yet Andi hadn't done a thing about her desire for Derrick. She hadn't even asked him out for coffee or drinks after work.

She held back a sigh. She didn't even know why she was thinking along this vein. Derrick would be a one-night-stand kind of man. She didn't do serious relationships, but she wasn't into one-nighters.

Of course he could go for what she wanted. Sex and lots of it with no ties.

Hmmm. Maybe she *would* go for it when she went back to work.

Shoving thoughts of Derrick out of her mind, Andi raised her chin and stepped out of the shadows. This was her weekend to find out what it was like to submit completely and turn over all control to a Dom.

A tremor of shock rolled through Andi and she froze. Across the room, a tall and powerfully built man stood with his back to her. He was talking to a diminutive blonde who was looking up at him with a sultry expression in her big green eyes.

Andi narrowed her gaze. It couldn't be—no. But that dark, wavy hair curling just above the collar of his coal gray suit jacket, those broad shoulders and strong hands . . .

No.

Andi took another drink of her Cosmo, finishing it off in one gulp. It couldn't be him. She set the empty martini glass on the bar and started to slink back into the shadows, but the man turned and his gaze met hers. Electricity zinged through Andi's body, straight to her sex.

It was him.

Derrick Macintyre.

Derrick's blood seared in his veins as his gaze rested on the beautiful, yet elusive, Andi Kelly. A slow smile curved in one corner of his mouth now that he had her attention. Andi's almond-shaped brown eyes widened and her lips parted in obvious surprise. She had a deer-trapped-in-headlights look about her as her gaze locked with his.

Dismissing his former sub without a backward glance, Derrick strode across the lounge, past club members, and straight toward Andi. She took a step back, as if she was about to turn and bolt from the room. He caught her by one wrist and pulled her to him.

Before she had a chance to speak, Derrick's gaze raked her from head to toe. He took in her shimmering curtain of black hair and could just imagine how it would feel sliding over his naked skin. The tiny black dress she wore showed her erect nipples rising beneath the thin material and the way it clung to the juncture of her thighs. His eyes traveled down long legs that wouldn't quit to a pair of sexy high heels. He couldn't wait to see her in nothing but those heels.

When his gaze met hers again, Andi tried to wrench her wrist from his grip. "I see you're just as much of an ass out of the boardroom as you are in," she said, her head raised and a determinedly haughty tilt to her chin.

Derrick drew her to him with a jerk and she lost her balance. With a soft gasp of surprise she fell against him, her slender body flush with his. He kept her pressed to him by gripping her ass with one hand. His erection was hard against her softness, and by the color rising in her cheeks he knew she hadn't had a problem noticing.

"As feisty as ever, Ms. Kelly." Derrick lowered his head and drank in Andi's jasmine perfume and her unique womanly scent. He had always loved how she smelled. From the first day he had met her, she had driven him out of his mind. "I think I'll punish you now."

Another soft gasp came from Andi and she tried to pull away from him. When he wouldn't release her, she tilted her head farther back, fire in her dark eyes. "Damn it, Macintyre." She stomped one high heel onto his shoe. "Let. Me. Go."

In a fast motion, Derrick released her wrist long enough to cup the back of her head. He clenched her silken hair in his fist and crushed his mouth to her soft lips, staking his claim, letting her know she was his for the weekend.

Andi tried to fight Derrick, her head swimming with shock. But he was too strong, too powerful.

His kiss was hard, almost brutal. Complete and total domination that took her breath away. She was so surprised that she parted her lips, and Derrick took advantage, thrusting his tongue into her mouth. He plunged hard and deep while he clenched his hand in her hair, a man in total control.

Without even realizing it was happening, Andi began kissing him back, letting her tongue dart into his mouth. Her fingers scaled his broad chest beneath his suit jacket and she rested her palms against him, feeling the flex of his hard muscles beneath her hands. His heat radiated through her and the image came to her of the two of them, hot and sweaty, slick flesh against slick flesh.

And she was moaning. Good God, she was *moaning*.

The fierceness of his kiss lessened, but he bit her lower lip hard enough to make her cry out. The pain quickly blended into a sweet kind of pleasure. Before she could recover from her surprise, he thrust his tongue deep inside her mouth again. He tasted of breath mints and the intoxicating flavor of pure male. His hand gripped her hair so hard she could feel it tugging against her scalp.

In that moment she could see herself submitting to Derrick. On her knees, doing whatever he wanted. Her hands tied behind her back while he fucked her mouth with his cock. Him taking her from behind, maybe even in her ass. Taking her any way he chose.

It seemed like the kiss lasted forever. When Derrick finally pulled back, her lips felt swollen and moist, her breath coming in soft gasps.

She couldn't take her gaze from his finely chiseled features, seeing the arrogant way one eyebrow rose as he watched her with those incredible blue eyes. The deep and throbbing sound of his voice made her panties damp when he said, "You're mine for the weekend, Andi." His jaw tightened and his face hardened with absolute seriousness. "You'll do what I say, when I say, and follow my instructions to the letter."

Andi started to shake her head, but his hand clenched her hair too tightly. "You bastard," she said. Heat rushed through her in a hot blaze. Yet part of her realized that it wasn't only anger flooding her, it was intense desire. His words had turned her on beyond belief.

"That'll earn you your first punishment." His gaze narrowed, his look turning darker. "Do you want to add another?"

Andi's jaw dropped. She couldn't believe this was happening. Derrick, here, at this exclusive BDSM club, and treating her like he was her Dom. And exciting her like no man had ever done before.

Derrick spoke before she could respond to his punishment remark. "Would you rather be a sub to a strange Dom? Would you rather be fucked by someone you don't know, Andi?" He brought her even tighter against him, digging his fingers hard into one ass cheek while clenching her hair in his other hand. He had her pressed so tightly against him that her hands and her breasts were smashed against his chest. "I won't let that happen," he continued. "I've wanted you, waited for you, for far too long to let another man have you."

Andi gulped. He'd wanted her? Had waited for her? He certainly had never shown it. "I—I don't know about this, Derrick. You—me—submitting . . ."

"Turn over control to me, baby." He relaxed his hold on her hair and ran his hand through it. The feel of his fingers skimming through her hair sent tingles of pleasure through her. "This weekend has nothing to do with the outside world. It has to do with you living your fantasy. And you pleasing me in any way I want you to."

Her eyes widened and her fingers clenched his shirt tighter. "How do you know it's my fantasy?"

"You're here." Derrick moved his finger to her lips, quieting her. "And it's obvious you've never been in a BDSM club before. You've stayed hidden in the shadows, clutching your drink like it was a shield. Admit it. You're here to experience what you've always dreamed about. I'm the man who's going to fulfill that fantasy."

Andi swallowed as she stared up at his blue eyes. Deep, endless blue, the color of the Caribbean. Between the Cosmo and her desire for Derrick, she was thoroughly intoxicated. She said the only thing she could say.

"Okay."

Chapter 2

Derrick's smile was absolutely carnal as he slowly released his hold on Andi. She found that she could breathe again, but her heart was still racing like crazy.

She straightened her spine. "Where do we start?" If she was going to do this, she was going to do it right.

He rubbed his hands up and down her bare arms and goose bumps roughened her skin. "Jamie will prepare you for me."

"Jamie?" Andi took her hands away from Derrick's chest. "Aren't you—I—"

He gestured behind her and Andi turned and gaped at the sight of a pretty redhead. The woman wore a tight red bustier with her ample breasts practically spilling from it. A short, snug red leather skirt molded her thighs, barely covering her mound, and she wore a pair of red high-heeled boots. But what grabbed Andi's attention was the red leather studded collar around her neck—and a D ring attached to it.

"Master Derrick." Jamie gave him a deep nod, snapping Andi's attention back to him.

"Please take Andi and get her ready for me." His gaze locked with Andi's and she gulped down a sudden rush of trepidation. "Put her into something tight and black that shows off her assets even better than what she's wearing." He reached up to trail his finger along Andi's jaw to her lips, never taking his gaze from hers. "But leave the heels."

Andi trembled, feeling aroused, excited, and frightened all at once. What had she gotten herself into?

Jamie bowed her head. "Yes, Master Derrick."

Derrick leaned over and murmured something to the redhead, then turned and strode away, leaving Andi alone with Jamie.

Andi watched him walk across the room, pushing his way through the crowd.

On second thought . . .

She took a step forward, feeling the sudden need to follow him. She had to tell him she'd changed her mind. She couldn't go through with this.

But Jamie reached out and took Andi by the hand. "Derrick is a good Master. You'll enjoy this weekend."

At that Andi's attention swung back to Jamie, a strange sense of jealousy surging through her at the thought of this woman being with Derrick. "Were you—are you—having a relationship with Derrick?"

Jamie laughed. "No. I have served only Master John for nine years. But you know how it is." She lowered her voice. "All the slaves talk. Derrick's got a reputation as a strict but fair Dom."

A sense of the surreal made Andi's head spin. This was a lifestyle for Derrick, not just a weekend thing?

"Let's get you ready." Jamie tugged at Andi's hand, escorting her around the corner from the bar, down a long, richly paneled hallway. The entire place was gorgeous, at least what she'd seen of it so far.

Andi allowed Jamie to lead her, not knowing what to say or do. *Crap, oh crap, oh crap. I don't know if I can do this.*

But she'd already told herself that she was going to go through with it. Too late to back out now.

Never letting go of Andi's hand, Jamie brought them to a stop in front of a huge mahogany door and rapped on it with her knuckles. When no one answered, Jamie ventured in with Andi in tow.

The door slammed shut behind them with a solid thunk. Andi's gaze took in a room that was as tastefully done as the lounge. It was a mixture of mahogany furnishings and walls, the furniture cushions and drapes done in royal blue and slate gray. It smelled of almonds and vanilla, and again Andi's stomach growled.

In the center of the room stood three massage tables upholstered in deep blue leather. Along one wall stood three stalls with drapes in royal blue, and next to them a door opened into a large walk-in closet filled with clothing packed too tightly together to see exactly what was in there. Leather, spandex, and that shiny black latex stuff, were about all she could define. Along another wall were mahogany cabinets and shelves holding a variety of bottles, containers, and strange-looking devices.

Mirrors covered the other two walls, and Andi's reflection stared back at her—a too-slender woman with small breasts, big brown eyes, and black hair in a sleek fall around a pale face.

The redhead swept her hand out to encompass the room. "This is where new slaves are prepared for their Masters."

Andi jerked her attention from the room to Jamie. "Slave? I'm going to be a sub for the weekend, not a slave."

The woman laughed and pointed toward one of the curtained

stalls. "Pick a changing room. Strip out of your clothing and put it into one of the bags. We'll have it sent to your room."

Andi could only stare at the woman, her heart beating faster than ever.

Jamie patted one of the massage tables. "When you're ready, lie down. You can wrap a towel around yourself if you want to."

You bet I do. "Is this all necessary?" Andi found herself twirling one of her fingers in a lock of her hair, something she hadn't done since she was a little girl.

"Sweetie, you're going to love it." Jamie took her by the arm and led her to the closest stall. "Just relax and turn over control. Stop worrying, and start enjoying."

Enjoy, enjoy, enjoy. God, the thought of turning over control seemed almost uplifting. She could do this. Right.

Andi slipped behind the heavy velvet curtain and into the dressing room. When she finished undressing, she shoved her clothing and heels into one of the fine cloth bags, then wrapped a thick blue towel around her body.

When she reentered the room, Jamie stood before the shelves, her back to Andi. "Go ahead and lie down, sweetie."

Andi held the towel tight around her as she climbed up onto one of the leather tables, face down.

"Jasmine." Jamie returned, carrying a bottle filled with golden oil. "Master Derrick insisted."

Andi frowned as Jamie poured some of the liquid into her hand and set the bottle down. Andi hadn't heard him say any such thing, although he *had* whispered to Jamie. It was a scent she loved, that she always wore, so she wasn't going to argue.

The air filled with jasmine perfume as Jamie rubbed the oil between her hands, then began massaging Andi's back with an experienced touch.

Andi couldn't help it. She groaned at the sensation of the woman working the oil into her body and relaxing the tension from her muscles. As Jamie worked, she pushed the towel down as she went, until Andi was naked. "Hey—" Andi started.

But Jamie said in a no-nonsense voice, "Better get used to baring yourself."

Andi gulped. "Okayyyy . . ."

While she massaged Andi's backside, Jamie explained the rules. "When you are in the same room as your Master, you have to keep your hands behind your back, your stance wide, and your gaze lowered."

Andi buried her face in her arms as Jamie rattled off more "rules." Oh, Andi had done her research on the Internet before coming to the Club, but the thought of actually going through with all this—with Derrick, no less—was scaring the hell out of her. This was no investment deal, nothing she was in control of.

As far as this weekend was concerned, she truly was going to be Derrick's slave.

Andi focused on the massage, trying not to tense up when Jamie kneaded her buttocks, then her upper thighs, nearing her folds. To her surprise, the intimate contact made Andi's folds ache. When Jamie had her turn over, it was even more so. Jamie's hands were skilled, professional, but as she worked over Andi's breasts, belly, and upper thighs Andi thought she'd scream if she didn't have an orgasm.

She was relieved when Jamie finally finished the sensual massage. She would have been mortified if she had climaxed.

Feeling boneless, Andi slid off the table with Jamie's help. She was entirely naked, but right now she didn't care. She felt too good, too relaxed.

"I have just the thing for you to wear for Master Derrick."

Jamie bustled to the closet and rummaged through it. When she returned, she was carrying a little black leather outfit that didn't look like it would cover much of anything.

It didn't. When Andi finally squeezed into the tight outfit in the changing booth, she stared at herself in the mirror, wide-eyed. The black leather corset tied below her breasts, thrusting the small globes up and together so that she actually had cleavage. It made her breasts look like they were on a serving platter. The top of the corset barely covered her nipples, a hint of her pink areolas peeking above the black leather.

The skirt wasn't much better, barely hiding the curls of her mound and her ass cheeks. There was no underwear.

"This can't be all of it," she said from the curtained changing booth.

"Let's see," came Jamie's pleasant voice from outside the booth. "Don't forget the heels."

"Heels. Right," Andi muttered as she riffled through the clothing bag and pulled out the four-inch black stilettos. She took another look in the full-length mirror. Her nipples rose up so hard and taut they could be seen pressing against the soft leather. The areolas puckered around the diamond-hard nubs that were barely concealed. Her cheeks were no longer pale, but flushed with either excitement or embarrassment—probably both—and her eyes were big, the irises a deep chocolate brown. Her hair hung in a dark shimmer over her shoulders, and she arranged it so that it spilled over her breasts, covering up what had been peeking out.

Damn, she looked hot. Talk about a sex kitten. Everything about how she was dressed and how she looked screamed, *Fuck me, I'm yours!*

Her cheeks burned at the thought of Derrick seeing her like

this. Maybe he'd take her right then and there, and relieve the ache between her thighs.

"Come on out, sweetie." Jamie sounded a trifle impatient. "Your Master is waiting."

Andi shivered. *Master.*

When she pushed aside the stall's curtain and stepped out into the room, her entire body burned. "There has got to be a wrap or something for this thing. I can't walk out there like this."

"It's perfect. Only one more thing." Jamie turned and rummaged in a cabinet, and then brought out a long strip of silver-studded black leather. "This should do."

Andi gulped when she saw that it was a collar, much like the one Jamie was wearing. It even had the D-ring to snap a leash to. "You are *not* going to put that thing on me."

Jamie sighed, her green eyes flashing with impatience. "Maybe Master Derrick would prefer to do it himself anyway. Some of the Doms do, you know."

Andi didn't know any such thing, but she'd wait and argue the point with Derrick.

Jamie escorted Andi from the room, down another hallway, to a common room filled with couples dressed a lot like her. Andi tried not to look at anyone as Jamie led her up a sweeping staircase to the second floor. The entire way Andi flushed with heat every time they passed anyone. From the corner of her eye, she noticed that both men and women gave her appreciative glances as they passed. But Andi kept her head up and tried not to meet anyone's eyes directly.

They passed numerous doors as Jamie led her forward. Everything was done beautifully in mahogany and forest green, and the carpet was paisley, done in the same deep green as well as burgundy.

They came to the end of another corridor, this one taking up an entire corner with a set of double doors, obviously a suite. Jamie knocked on the immense mahogany doors, and Andi held her breath.

Chapter 3

The moment Derrick heard the knock at the door his gut tightened. He had bided his time, waiting for his opportunity with Andi. At the investment corporation she was always so cool and aloof—untouchable. But now he was going to do more than touch. His cock strained against his leather pants, and he wondered how long he was going to last before he had to take her.

No, he was going to make her wait as long as possible.

With slow, even strides, he walked toward the door of the spacious suite, knowing that every moment of anticipation would heighten Andi's nervousness and desire. It was going to take all his strength not to fuck her the moment he saw her.

He didn't realize how true that thought was until he swung the door open and saw Andi standing in the hallway, her chin raised and her eyes flashing with the spunk and fire he had always admired in her.

Yes, this weekend was going to be interesting.

"Master Derrick, her collar." Jamie handed it to him, then bowed her head. "If you have nothing else . . ."

He waved her off, unable to take his gaze from Andi. "Thank you, Jamie."

The slave strolled away, leaving Andi and Derrick alone in the hallway. Clenching the collar in his fist, he took a moment to drink in the sight of her, letting her nervousness build as he appreciated every damn inch of her. Jamie had picked out the perfect outfit, the tight leather skirt so short it revealed Andi's mile-long legs, and the corset pushed up her luscious breasts in a way that made his fingers itch to touch them.

Derrick took Andi's hand and drew her into the room. Her fingers trembled in his grasp despite the composed and haughty expression on her face.

Oh yeah, he was going to enjoy teaching her to submit.

When they were alone in the room, Derrick said, "I'm sure Jamie taught you the rules. You've decided to ignore the first. Lower your eyes."

Andi bit her bottom lip and he could see the war within her. A take-charge woman giving over control to a dominant man— she was obviously going to need to be taught a lesson. Likely several.

Inwardly he smiled at the thought.

When Andi didn't answer immediately, he said, "Do you need a second punishment, too?"

After a brief flare of defiance in her brown eyes, Andi lowered her gaze and bowed her head. "No . . . Master." She widened her stance and put her hands behind her back.

He slowly walked around Andi, trailing the leather collar over her shoulders and back, admiring every beautiful inch of his woman. She smelled of jasmine oil and the rich scent of her desire.

He stopped behind her and skimmed the collar along the inside of one thigh, up and under the skirt toward her mound. Andi made a small gasp, but to her credit didn't move. His hand slowly traveled up to her folds, where he cupped her pussy, pressing the leather against her softness. He slid one finger into her silky wetness and she shuddered.

"You're ready for me." He stroked her clit and Andi let out a small groan as more of her moisture coated his hand. "Do you want me to make you come now?"

Andi's voice was low and breathless when she responded, "Yes."

"Yes . . . what?"

"Yes, Master."

He paused for a moment, letting the anticipation build. "No, I don't think you've earned that." He slipped his fingers from her folds and brought his hand to his nose to drink in her heady scent. His cock twitched. Damn, at this rate, *he* wasn't going to last long.

When he finished circling Andi and stood in front of her again, he said, "Raise your head."

Andi obeyed and thrust her breasts out so that they were displayed in a way that made *his* knees weak. But still, her long, dark hair obscured his view.

Desire seared Andi's veins as Derrick pushed her hair behind her shoulders. Her folds still tingled from where he had stroked them, and she was just dying for an orgasm.

He looked so damn good in a black sleeveless T-shirt and tight leather pants that molded his athletic thighs. He smelled good, too. Of spicy aftershave and male musk.

After he pushed back her hair, Derrick used the black collar to trace the top of the corset, over each breast, stroking the dark pink of her areolas that peeked above the material. He hooked one finger at the middle of the corset, and Andi gasped as he tugged and her breasts popped free.

"Beautiful," he murmured, rubbing the collar from one taut nipple to the other. He lowered his head and flicked his tongue over each pebble-hard nub. Andi couldn't help the soft moan that spilled through her lips at the contact.

A knock came at the door and Derrick raised his head. His gaze locked with hers for one long moment. "Don't move," he commanded, and turned to walk toward the door.

Andi brought her hands in front of her and started to tug the corset up and over her breasts before he opened the door. Derrick glanced at her when his hand rested on the door handle.

"I told you to not move." He gave her a firm look as he stuffed the collar into a pocket of his leather pants. "You've just earned your second punishment."

"But—"

"Do you want to earn a third?" His gaze narrowed. "Don't speak unless I say you can, and put your hands behind your back and your stance wide. Leave the corset under your breasts so that I can see them."

Andi thought about arguing, but wasn't too sure what he had in mind for her punishments. She decided to obey and put her hands behind her back and lowered her gaze.

When Derrick opened the door, he let in three men carrying domed platters and she watched them from under her lashes. Andi thought she was going to die of embarrassment, standing there with her naked breasts on display. A swirl of air came in from the hall, brushing over her nipples, making them ache even more.

To her relief, the waiters didn't look at her. They busied themselves with setting down the trays, lifting domes, and arranging food upon the large mahogany table at one end of the room.

Andi's stomach growled even louder this time as she caught the rich smells of lobster, shrimp, grilled salmon, clam chowder, and fresh-baked bread.

To get her mind off food, and off her naked breasts, she gazed at her surroundings from beneath her lashes. It was an absolutely amazing suite, with richly polished mahogany furnishings and the cushions done in cranberry velvet. Vases of fresh flowers graced the tables, in what must be the sitting room. Andi caught the perfume of roses, orchids, and lilies mixed with the scent of lemon oil.

To the far end of the room was another set of double doors, and Andi imagined it led to the bedroom. Just the thought of going into the bedroom with Derrick sent more thrills through her pussy. God, was she really going to fuck her fellow VP?

When the men finally left, the door slammed shut behind them. Derrick moved to Andi, his movements lithe and graceful. She had never seen him in anything but his expensively tailored business suits, and she couldn't believe he looked even hotter in just a sleeveless T-shirt and those leather pants and black boots he'd changed into.

He paused at a wardrobe with two drawers at its base, and a pair of doors that swung open when he grabbed the handles. Several shelves lined the right side of the wardrobe, an assortment of items littering each shelf. On the left side, a few outfits hung— very sexy-looking outfits from what she could tell.

When Derrick closed the wardrobe, he had a tube in one hand and something that looked like a black leather belt with a dildo and a butt plug on it. . . .

Oh, shit.

Andi swallowed, hard, and she forgot about not looking up. Her eyes seemed to grow wider and wider the closer he came. "Uh, you're not—"

"Andi . . ." He frowned. "You know you're not allowed to talk without permission."

She swallowed again. "Yes, Master."

He stroked hair from her face. "And no, you don't have permission." He knelt before her and pressed the inside of one of her knees. "Lower your gaze again and spread your legs wider."

Andi obeyed, half afraid and half excited about what she knew he was about to do.

"This is your first punishment." He used the gel from the tube and lubed the butt plug so that it glistened in the room's soft lighting. He pushed up her skirt and grabbed one of her ass cheeks with one hand. "You'll wear this belt until I let you remove it."

Andi held her breath as he placed the head of the plug at the puckered flesh of her anus. Slowly he entered her, gently pushing the plug up her ass, filling her deeply. She had to bite her lip to keep from moaning with pleasure.

He leaned forward and his tongue darted out, snaking along her slit, and more moisture flooded her as a thrill curled through her belly.

"You're so hot and wet." His voice held a note of satisfaction.

Definitely no need to lube the dildo part.

Derrick thrust the rubber cock into her channel and Andi gasped at the sudden intrusion. She almost moved her hands from behind her back to brace herself against his shoulders, but managed to catch herself in time.

He fastened around her waist the leather harness that kept the dildo and the plug tight in her orifices. She'd never felt anything like it in her life, and she thought she'd come if she took a single step.

As if reading her mind, his blue eyes met hers as he straightened and said, "You can't come without my permission. Do you understand?"

Well, damn. She hesitated, but he narrowed his gaze and she hurried to say, "Yes, Master."

Derrick turned and strode to the table covered with delicious-smelling food, and seated himself. She waited for him to tell her to sit down at the table, but instead he began filling his plate, ignoring her. She started to say something but snapped her mouth shut. Her stomach did the talking for her, growling so loudly she'd just about bet it could have been heard through the heavy doors and into the hallway.

When his plate was full, he finally looked at her. "Stand here." He pointed to the carpet directly in front of him.

Andi kept her hands behind her back and followed his instructions. With the plug up her ass, and the dildo up her pussy, she felt like she was waddling. It was hard to walk in stilettos and look graceful when her orifices were stuffed with rubber.

When she reached him, he said, "Kneel."

She only hesitated a moment, then knelt before him, feeling the shift and pull of the plugs within her.

He withdrew the studded black collar from his pocket and held it in front of her. "You're my slave for the weekend, Andi, and you'll wear my collar." The tone of his voice said he wouldn't accept any kind of argument.

She gritted her teeth. "Yes, Master."

He adjusted her long hair so that he could fasten the collar around her neck. When he finished he caught her chin in his hand. "You belong to me this weekend."

Shivers of excitement at his tone and the look in his eyes shuddered through her. "Yes, Master," she whispered.

"But, you do need a safe word." His expression became serious as he spoke. "If anything frightens you or is beyond what you can handle, you'll say your safe word and the weekend is over."

Andi swallowed. *Safe word . . . safe word . . .*

"Monaco," she blurted out.

Derrick laughed. "That'll work."

Derrick turned back to his dinner. A margarita glass was set before his plate, with chilled shrimp around the rim. He dipped one into the red sauce in the middle of the glass and brought the shrimp to her mouth. "Eat."

She parted her lips and took a bite of the giant shrimp. The tang of lemon and the sinus-clearing taste of horseradish filled her mouth along with the succulent shrimp. Keeping his eyes fixed on hers, he brought the shrimp to his mouth and took a bite from it before dipping it into the sauce and feeding it to her again.

While he fed her, he brushed the fingers of his free hand across her bare nipples. She moaned around the bite of food. Between the plug in her ass, the dildo in her pussy, and the way he was feeding her, stroking her, she could climax right then.

The bastard knew exactly what he was doing.

Chapter 4

With Andi on her knees, Derrick had a hard time not showing his satisfaction in her submissiveness. How many times had he fantasized about this moment? Countless.

Every time Andi took a bite of food from his hand, her soft mouth would suck lightly at his fingers, and he had to fight to keep back his own groans. She looked so beautiful with her breasts on display, staring up at him with those gorgeous, deep brown eyes.

As far as Derrick was concerned, the meal lasted far too long. But he was pleased to see Andi squirming at his feet, and he had to remind her that she didn't have his permission to climax.

When he had fed each of them the last bite of dinner, he said, "Time for dessert." He pushed his plate away and reached for a slice of Key lime pie. He reached down to twist a finger in her hair and tugged at it. "For you, too."

Andi gasped as he yanked her hair a little harder, drawing her closer to him, allowing her to feel the pain and the pleasure of his control over her. He widened his thighs and brought her so that her face was close to his crotch, where his cock strained to get through his pants.

When he had her where he wanted her, Derrick released her hair and unfastened his leather pants, zipping them all the way down. The pants had a zipper that went below his balls, allowing him total freedom.

Andi's eyes widened and her tongue darted along her lower lip. He stroked his erection in front of her mouth, the head of his shaft almost touching her lips.

Derrick picked up the dessert plate and held it close to her. "Take the pie filling and spread it on my cock with your fingers."

Andi's face flushed a pretty shade of pink as she dipped two fingers into the dessert and scooped out some of the filling. He released his erection and watched as she spread the filling up and down his length. Damn, her hand felt good on him, and he couldn't wait to have her hot mouth sliding over his cock.

"Until it's covered," he said when she finished spreading what was on her fingers.

Andi scooped more pie filling out and concentrated on coating his shaft until no bare skin remained. His voice nearly came out in a growl as he said, "Lick it off."

Her tongue darted out as she flicked it over the head of his cock, and he almost shuddered at the pleasure of it. It was all he could do to not allow his eyes to roll back in his head. She continued, slowly swiping her tongue up and down his length, licking and sucking every bit of the Key lime pie filling. He was certain she was teasing him, taunting him, maybe to get even for the dildos. She even went down to his sac and licked the balls that were as hard as walnuts from wanting her so badly.

When she finished cleaning the dessert from his erection, he said, "Suck my cock."

Without hesitation, Andi went down on him. He clenched his fist in her silken black hair and guided her as she sucked him off. She made little humming noises that about drove him out of his mind. "That's it, baby," he said as she moved up and down, working his shaft with her hand while her tongue flicked along his length. "Don't stop for a second."

Damn. He wasn't going to be able to last. "I'm going to come in your sweet little mouth, and you're going to swallow every drop." Her eyes met his, and she gave him a questioning look as she continued to suck.

"Come on, baby." He massaged the back of her head. "You can do it."

Andi sucked harder. "That's it. Just like that." He fought to keep his eyes open so he could watch his erection sliding in and out of her mouth. He began pumping his hips in rhythm with her motions.

His climax built up within him, a raging inferno that took him like a firestorm. He bit the inside of his cheek to keep from crying out as his cock jerked and his semen shot into Andi's mouth. She didn't pause. Instead she sucked harder as she swallowed every drop of his come.

When he couldn't take it any longer, he fisted his hand in her hair and pulled her away from him. His moist cock slid out of her mouth and he gritted his teeth to retain control.

Shit. He'd never had such a mind-bending blowjob in all his life. He could swear he'd seen stars behind his eyes.

Andi licked her lips, swallowing the last of Derrick's come. She'd never swallowed before and she was surprised to find she enjoyed it. It had been the connection between her and Derrick that made the experience even more intimate. He had tasted salty-sweet, mixed with the flavor of the delicious Key lime pie. She had enjoyed licking off every last bit of it.

She also loved the look in Derrick's eyes right now. Dark, and burning with passion. Her pussy throbbed and she wanted his cock there instead of the dildo. She wanted him to take her in the ass, too, instead of the butt plug that filled her.

He stood and tucked himself back into his leather pants. After he zipped up, he held his hand out to her and helped her rise to her feet. Her bare nipples brushed his T-shirt and she felt the heat of him emanating throughout her body.

"So good, Andi." He took her hand and led her to the double doors across the room. "You have a talented mouth."

"Thank you, Master," she murmured.

The dildo and butt plug stimulated her with every movement she made, and she desperately hoped he was going to remove them and then fuck her out of her mind.

Her stomach fluttered as he opened the doors, revealing a huge four-poster bed, along with beautiful furnishings. The tingling in her belly grew even more intense as she thought about Derrick taking her in that bed.

The plush burgundy carpet sank beneath her heels and a light breeze stirred by an overhead fan brushed across her skin.

When they reached the center of the room, Derrick stopped and released her hand. "Kneel."

She assumed the position. The plugs in her pussy and ass seemed to sink in even further, and she bit the inside of her lip to hold back a moan. She could just imagine how she looked from behind, that little black skirt not hiding a damn thing.

She heard Derrick rustling behind her and then, the next thing she knew, he was kneeling beside her, trailing a black silk scarf over her cheek.

"I'm going to blindfold you now, baby." His tone was low and sexy. She liked the way he called her "baby." It was such a sensual endearment coming from his lips.

Derrick slipped the blindfold over her eyes and tied it securely behind her head. It was so dark that other senses sharpened. She heard rustling again as he moved away from her. She heard the sound of her own breathing, Derrick's soft footfalls on the carpet, and the gentle *whoosh* of air from the overhead fan. She caught the freshly shampooed carpet smell and the scent of her juices.

When she heard Derrick moving back toward her, all her senses came on full alert. A tingling sensation skittered along her spine and she shivered. God, she wished she could see.

Derrick's strong hands gripped each of her ass cheeks and she startled. He gently kneaded the flesh as he spoke in a soft, reassuring voice, but what he said didn't reassure her at all.

"Baby, you know I have to punish you now." He continued massaging her buttocks as he spoke, but her *what-am-I-doing-here* ratio doubled.

"With the dildo and butt plug you've been punished for calling me 'bastard' earlier, instead of 'Master.'" She thought she heard amusement in his voice, but she was probably imagining it. "Now you'll be punished for moving when I told you to stay still. Do you understand?"

"Yes," she whispered.

"Andi . . ." he said in a warning tone.

"Master. Yes, Master."

He continued stroking her, and speaking to her in the patient

I-am-God tone. "I'll have to punish you the next time you forget to call me Master."

Andi dug her fingers into the carpet to keep control of herself. This was turning out to be harder than she'd imagined. "Yes, Master."

"Good." He moved his hands away from her and she felt something gentle sliding over her skin. It was different than the scarf that covered her eyes. This felt like soft strips of suede that tickled her skin and made her shiver.

"Do you know what this is?" Derrick trailed it over her ass and down between her thighs, causing more moisture to wet the dildo in her pussy.

She thought about it a moment, and then a little bubble of fear and curiosity rose up within her. "A—a flogger?"

"Yeah." He continued to slide the flogger over her skin, up to her neck, along her spine, and down again to her ass cheeks. "You've been a bad girl, Andi Kelly, and you have to be punished."

Oh shit, oh shit, oh shit. What had she gotten herself into?

Her body was unbelievably tense as he continued to stroke her, drawing out the moment when he would flog her. "I'm going to punish you for teasing me all this time in the boardroom. For making me want you."

In the next moment all thought fled her mind as the flogger met her flesh in a hard swat. Andi cried out, but barely had time to register the first when the second swat fell. It stung. It hurt like hell. Every swat was even more intense because she was blindfolded.

Then the pain began to take on a pleasurable feeling. It started to blend with the sensations she was feeling in her ass and in her pussy. Every swat heightened her arousal and she started to squirm.

"Quiet, baby." He swatted her harder and she jerked forward. "I can't stop until you're completely silent."

Andi shook and bit the inside of her cheek so hard she almost cried out from the pain of it. The metallic taste of blood was in her mouth, but she didn't care—it only added to all the other things she was feeling.

With the blindfold on, it intensified *all* the sensations, making everything seem so much more extreme. Her thighs trembled and her stomach clenched as she felt the beginning of a major orgasm coming on.

"Don't climax," he said, as if reading her mind. He swatted her again even harder. "Hold back or you'll earn a worse punishment."

Shit. What could be worse?

She didn't want to know.

He kept flogging her. Her ass stung and her cheek burned from where she was biting it. She started to see stars behind the black blindfold as wave after wave of pleasure soared through her, bringing her closer and closer to that brink she wasn't supposed to cross.

And then he swatted her hard enough to send her over the edge. Andi screamed. Her body jerked and she rolled onto her side. She was barely conscious of anything around her. It seemed like her entire world had exploded. More stars burst in her head. Her pussy throbbed around the dildo, and her anus kept contracting around the plug. Her entire body was one big, massive orgasm, and she thought it would never end.

As she began to come down from the high, she heard Derrick sigh before he said, "Baby, you've just earned one hell of a punishment."

Chapter 5

At that moment, Andi couldn't care less what kind of punishment Derrick had in mind for her. She'd just had the most amazing orgasm of her life. She had no other way to describe it. Just *amazing*.

She was on her side, panting, aftershocks still clenching and unclenching around the dildo in her core and plug in her ass. Her butt stung like crazy and her blindfold had scooted up so that she could now see out of one eye. Her leather outfit stuck to her skin from all the sweat, and she felt a trickle of perspiration roll by one eye. She was so limp, so completely sated, that a truck could have rumbled through the room and she wouldn't have been able to move.

But then something—er, someone—more frightening than a Mack truck bent down in front of her with a *you-are-so-in-for-it-now* look on his strong features. "Get up, Andi," he said in a calm tone, and he pulled the blindfold the rest of the way off so she could see him clearly. Damn, he looked *mad*.

She forced herself to a sitting position, which was no easy feat at all. Her limbs trembled and she just wanted to lie back in a puddle on the incredibly soft and deep carpet.

With some effort she managed to get to her feet and almost stumbled in her heels.

"Come," Derrick said as he turned and strode away from her.

Andi grinned behind his back. *I just did.*

She quickly smothered the grin and hurried to follow him. She just about moaned again as the dildo and plug moved within her still-quivering body. Her ass wouldn't stop stinging, which didn't help the urge to have countless more orgasms.

He strode toward another set of doors and pushed them open to the poshest bathroom Andi had ever seen. Her own room at the exclusive resort was nice, but could have fit in that bathroom. Acres of beautiful Italian tile, more mahogany cabinets and marble countertops, and vases of fresh flowers. An enormous whirl-pool tub occupied one corner of the bathroom and looked as though it could seat at least four couples. Around it plants spilled down ledges built into the wall so that it looked as if the spa was in a tropical forest.

Derrick walked around a marble wall that flowed from cabinets to spa and Andi saw it was a large shower with three shower-heads. There were also large, unusual-looking hooks built into the shower, away from the showerheads, and Andi wondered what they were for.

When she reached him, Derrick held out the scarf that he had used for a blindfold. "Put out your wrists."

"Yes, Master," she murmured as contritely as possible.

Derrick quickly tied her wrists and then forced her back against the wall, beneath one of the hooks. He raised her arms and caught the scarf on the hook so that she was practically dangling from it. Her breasts thrust up and obviously caught Derrick's attention at once. He pinched and tugged at both her nipples, and rolled them between his thumb and forefinger, hard enough to cause her to gasp.

"My bad, bad girl," he murmured, his blue eyes fixed on her. "What should I do with you?"

"Is that a rhetorical question, um, Master?" She bit her lip, hoping he wouldn't catch her slip at speaking without permission.

He reached for the ties of her corset and began to unlace them. "This isn't the boardroom, baby. There are no negotiations here. You do as I say, you serve me and see to it that I'm having a real good time. That's your goal. Do you understand?"

Andi nodded. "Yes, Master."

Derrick focused on unfastening her corset and tossed it aside, leaving her naked from the waist up. But then he unzipped her skirt, letting it drop around her ankles until she was clad only in the leather dildo harness and her stilettos, the leather collar still around her neck.

"You look delicious just like that." He ran his finger from between her breasts down to the harness around her waist. "But we don't want to ruin the leather or your shoes, so we'll just have to lose them."

He removed the collar, and Andi felt strangely naked without it—even though she was already naked. *Like that makes sense.*

His talented fingers roamed her body, teasing and tantalizing her as he slowly unhooked the harness. Andi almost cried out in relief. Yet she felt a sudden emptiness at the loss of stimulation when the dildo and butt plug were removed, too.

Next he bent down and took off her stilettos, massaging each foot after removing the shoe. When he finished, she was dangling from the hook, her toes barely touching the cool tile floor. Her arms ached from being over her head. She felt suddenly small and vulnerable, from the way he was standing there, fully clothed, and watching her with a dark look on his well-cut features.

Derrick folded his arms across his chest and studied Andi's delicious body. Her long black hair hung straight down her back and her slim body begged for his touch. He'd once heard her say she was too skinny, but he thought she was out of her mind. She was perfect.

His gaze traveled over her small, firm breasts, down to her narrow waist, and on to the triangle of dark hair between her thighs. And damn, her legs—he'd always loved her long legs.

Yeah, he had her right where he'd always wanted her.

Derrick stripped out of his T-shirt, kicked off his boots, and shucked off his leather pants. All the while, Andi's gaze never wavered. Her eyes widened at the sight of his erect cock, which jerked against his belly when her tongue flicked out and moistened her lips in a deliberate and inviting way.

Yeah, she was a very bad girl. And he was going to enjoy every minute of her punishment.

He brushed by Andi as he stepped past her into the shower, and she gave a soft gasp as his arm roughened her nipples.

He ran the water until it was at a comfortably warm temperature, then unhooked the showerhead and began spraying Andi's skin with it, avoiding her hair, before setting the showerhead aside again.

Derrick grabbed a cloth and soaped it with jasmine-scented gel. "You have such a beautiful body," he said as he began washing her. He started at her neck, and she tipped her head back and gave a soft moan.

Slowly he worked his way down her body, carefully soaping

every inch of her. Andi moaned again as he washed her breasts and made sure her nipples were more than sensitized.

"Is this my punishment, Master?" Andi asked, her voice breathless as he reached the soft curls of her mound.

"Not even close." He slipped one finger into her folds and stroked her clit, and liked how she trembled.

Andi knew Derrick was intentionally driving her crazy. God, it felt so good having him wash her body. She wished her hands were free so that she could touch him and wash his powerful body the same way he was washing hers. She loved the way his muscles rippled across his back as he moved, the flex of his biceps, the concentration on his masculine features. Part of her still couldn't believe she was actually here at the Club, Derrick's slave for the weekend.

Boy, this ought to make for some interesting board meetings once they went back to reality.

When he finished soaping her body, Derrick set aside the rag and again took the showerhead. He rinsed away the soap, rubbing his palms over her skin as he went. He stopped to palm her breasts, and Andi squirmed from his sensual touch. But when he reached her still-sensitized clit, he stroked it even harder than before, and she nearly lost it.

"Spread your legs." He pushed at the insides of her thighs as he spoke.

"Yes, Master." Andi did the best she could, considering she was hanging from a hook and her toes barely touched the shower floor.

Derrick pulled apart the lips of her pussy with one hand and brought the showerhead between her thighs. Andi cried out at the feel of the pulsating jets of water against her folds. She could feel another orgasm building, and she was willing to bet that it would be a powerful one.

As she started to tremble, Derrick moved the showerhead away from her, and her body sagged at the sudden loss of stimulation.

"Andi . . ." His voice was full of reproach as he stood and forced her to turn so that her back was to him. Fortunately, the way he had knotted the scarf and placed it on the hook managed to keep her wrists from hurting. But her body was another story. She ached from hanging for so long and she was beginning to feel light-headed.

"I love your hair," Derrick said after he turned her so that her back was to him. He sifted his fingers through her hair and Andi sighed at the luxurious feel of it. "Do you know how many times I've imagined you naked, riding me, with your hair sliding across my skin?"

Wow. She'd had no idea. "Really? I mean no, Master."

"I have, baby." He continued running his fingers through her hair in a way that made her want to moan. "But that's not all I've imagined."

He left her for one moment, and in the next she heard the shower spray and warm water rush through her hair. When it was wet, he began shampooing her hair, massaging her scalp as he did so.

"I've imagined you tied up in my bed while I fucked you out of your mind." His massage intensified at the same time that Andi's sex grew wetter from his words. "I've imagined you here, walking naked beside me through the resort while other men admired your body, knowing no one else would ever touch you but me . . . or anyone I want to touch you."

Andi stilled. "You wouldn't make me do that, would you?"

"You've earned yourself another punishment, baby." He began rinsing the soap from her hair. "You spoke without permission and you didn't address me like you're supposed to."

Andi sagged against her bonds. "I'm sorry, Master."

"I can't let you get away with it. You do understand, don't you?"

She sighed. "Yes, Master."

"Good." He turned her to face him again and reached up to untie the scarf holding her to the hook.

When he released her, he massaged her aching arms down to her wrists and smiled at her. "It's your turn to wash me."

With pleasure. "Yes, Master."

She used the showerhead on him, enjoying how the water beaded and rolled off his tanned skin. When she had finished, she soaped him thoroughly, exploring every inch of his sexy body. She wanted to fuck him so badly, to rake her nails down his back, and to sink her teeth into his shoulder. She wanted it hard and fast and wild.

When she reached his erection, she was on her knees and she wanted to slide her mouth over him again, to taste him. But when she looked up at him, he shook his head no.

Andi let out a little sigh and continued washing his legs, then moved behind him to scrub his thighs. After she rinsed him off, she washed his hair. It wasn't easy considering how much taller he was, but she managed.

When they were finished showering, Derrick toweled them both off, then led her naked to a vanity in the bathroom where he combed out her hair. She burned with desire as she studied his nude reflection and the concentration on his dark, handsome features. It was such an intimate moment and she felt a flutter in her heart.

Once her hair hung down her back, every tangle combed from it, Derrick raked his fingers through his own hair, giving it a sexy, mussed look, before taking her back into the bedroom.

"Tomorrow you'll be punished for climaxing before I said you could." He led her to the bed. For one moment Andi felt excitement at being able to cuddle up next to Derrick while they slept, but then he knelt down and pulled a trundle bed out from under the much larger bed.

Her heart fell and her gaze shot to Derrick.

"I'm sorry, baby, but you disobeyed. You'll sleep here tonight, and tomorrow, if you've earned it, you can sleep in bed with me."

Andi just stared at him. The bastard! But when his eyes darkened, she swallowed her anger and said, "Yes, Master."

She eased herself down onto the bed and beneath the covers. He knelt beside her and brushed a kiss over her forehead. "Don't try to climax tonight." He lightly stroked her shoulder through the blanket. "I'll know and you'll earn another punishment."

Andi nearly groaned as he moved away. There went that idea.

Chapter 6

Derrick woke to sunshine sliding through the wooden slats of the bedroom's mahogany blinds. Propping himself on one elbow, he peered over the side of the bed to where Andi was sleeping and studied her.

What a beautiful woman. Her black hair was wild around her head, strands of it lying across her face and along the curve of her neck. Her eyes were closed, her lashes dark against her fair skin. The comforter was draped over her hips, and his cock hardened at the sight of one breast and its puckered nipple. A slight sigh escaped her full lips and she stirred, rubbing her thighs together as if she needed to come even in her sleep.

He smiled at the thought of what he had planned for her today. She was spirited and fiery, and not one to back down from a challenge. The fact that she was submitting to him was amazing.

Derrick studied Andi and imagined just how good things were going to be today. He'd wanted her for so long. He'd imagined fucking her so many times he'd had to take care of that need in other ways.

He hadn't asked her out yet because he wanted to get to know her a little better . . . and draw out both of their needs as long as possible. For him, part of being a Dom who wanted a particular woman was knowing when the time was right to make his move—he'd had to wait to make her want him so much that she'd do anything for him.

Now he had her.

But he'd wanted more from her than just sex, and thanks to Sheila Tassoni, he knew Andi wasn't into long-term relationships. Once Sheila had caught him watching Andi, and Sheila had said in a soft voice, "Never push Andi if you want more than sex. She'll push back and won't let you in."

He'd wondered how he could be that transparent when he did all he could to be just the opposite.

Yeah, he wanted more. He admired more than Andi's beauty. He loved her smile, the way she worked with others, her sense of humor, and her fire. He loved to see her eyes spark when they went toe to toe and so many times he'd just wanted to grab her by her shoulders and kiss her. Hard. He wanted to possess her—because in a way she possessed him.

Just how much, he didn't think he was ready to admit, especially to himself.

Derrick didn't know how long he had watched her—drinking in the sight of her, when her eyelids fluttered open. She looked slightly dazed and confused when she first looked up at him, but then the prettiest blush stole over her cheeks.

"Good morning, baby," he said softly.

She covered her mouth as she gave a little yawn. "Morning, Derr—um, Master."

"Good girl." He slid out of bed, letting the blanket and sheet slide down his nude body. Andi's eyes widened, her gaze fixed on his mammoth erection. This was going to be hell, making her wait, making himself wait. But it was going to be so damn good when he finally did take her.

Derrick went to the wardrobe as she pushed herself up in the small bed.

"I have something I'd like you to wear today."

Andi raked her fingers through her hair, her eyes still heavy-lidded from sleep. "Yes, Master," she mumbled as she eased to her feet and moved to him. She walked as though she ached. He barely kept from smiling. She was going to be so on edge today that, by the time he fucked her, it was going to be one hell of an orgasm for both of them.

When she reached him, Derrick asked, "Did you enjoy the harness yesterday?"

Andi tilted her head as she looked up at him. "Do you want me to answer honestly, Master?"

He nodded. "Of course."

"It drove me out of my mind, Master." She ran her hands down her waist to her thighs. "I need to come so bad I could just scream."

Derrick almost laughed. "That's the idea. Part of your punishment."

Andi sighed. "Yes, Master."

"My concern now," he said as he partially turned to the wardrobe, "is today's punishment for climaxing without permission last night."

A worried expression crossed Andi's beautiful features, but to her credit she didn't say anything.

He withdrew a lingerie box from the cabinet that contained

something special he had purchased just for Andi when she'd arranged the weekend. When Shelia Tassoni had "let it slip" that Andi would be here, Derrick had made sure she would be his for the weekend.

He handed the elegant box to Andi. "I'd like to see you in this."

Raising an eyebrow, she took the box and moved to the bed, where she set it down and opened it. Wrapped in tissue paper were a leather push-up bra, a leather G-string, and a diamond-studded leather collar—along with a leash.

Andi's heart sank as she pulled the leash from the box. *Oh. My. God.* He was actually going to leash her.

She cut her gaze to him and he gave her that devastatingly sexy smile of his. "Put on the clothing, baby."

"This is not what I call clothing," Andi muttered.

Derrick raised an eyebrow. "Excuse me?"

"Nothing, Master." Andi dropped her gaze to the clothing. "I'll just slip into these . . . things." She gestured to the bathroom. "I need to use the facilities. Can I just change in there?"

He gave a deep nod. "Don't forget the heels. They're still in the bathroom, near the shower. Use anything you want. They're here just for you."

Andi swore he was trying to hide a smile. The bastard was getting a kick out of this. She'd kick him. . . .

She gathered up the box of leather nothings and scooted into the bathroom before he changed his mind. She closed the large mahogany door behind her, then leaned up against it.

Oh, shit. She was in for it today, she just knew it.

After she finished with the facilities and freshened up, she used the comb Derrick had used on her hair last night to fluff it out. It hung like dark, shining silk over her bare shoulders, and slid across her naked back like a caress. She found new packages of lip gloss and blusher sitting on the vanity, which was all she ever used anyway, and assumed that's what Derrick had meant when he told her to make herself at home.

When she had finished touching up, she slipped on the minuscule leather G-string and cringed. *Crap.* He wasn't going to make her go out in public like this, was he?

Next came the push-up bra that made her breasts rise up so high and close they looked like they were airborne. She found her heels exactly where they'd left them last night, and by the time she had them on she was sure she looked like a stripper or, worse yet, a hooker.

Lastly, she pulled out the collar that had a D ring attached, then withdrew the leash from the box. They were made from the same supple black leather as the G-string and the bra, and felt soft against her hand.

Taking a deep breath, she clenched both in her fist. Maybe if she gave him big puppy-dog eyes, he'd forgo the torture?

Yeah, right.

While Andi was preparing herself, Derrick dressed. Breakfast arrived and was set up in the suite. He smiled to himself as he remembered Andi's embarrassment the night before, when dinner was served and she was wearing virtually nothing.

Smells of sausage, scrambled eggs, and pancakes filled the room, along with Andi's lingering scent.

When she finally pushed open the bathroom door and slipped into the bedroom, Derrick just about came in his leather pants. Her chin was high, her black hair flowing about her shoulders, and she had a light tint of blush to her cheeks and gloss to her lips. But hell, it was her body that about made him drop to his knees. The G-string and heels made her legs look longer than ever, and that bra—God, he just wanted to rip it off and eat her up.

He gritted his teeth, trying to tame his erection but not having a whole hell of a lot of luck with it. He'd dressed in snug black leather pants and a leather lace-up shirt, both in the same soft leather as Andi's sexy outfit.

His voice came out gravelly when he spoke, and he mentally kicked himself. "The collar?"

Andi's expression fell as she raised her hand. "Here, Master."

He motioned to her to come to him, and his cock ached at the sway of her hips and the bounce of her breasts in their tiny leather slingshots.

He slipped the collar from her hand. "Turn around, baby."

"Yes, Master," Andi said quietly as she obeyed.

He pushed her hair over one shoulder and wrapped the soft diamond-and-leather collar around her neck. When he turned her back around, the platinum D ring glowed in the sunshine spilling through the blinds. He took the leash from her hand and saw the glint of fire in her eyes as he raised the clasp to her neck. One cheek was sucked in, and he was certain she was biting the inside of it to keep from telling him exactly where he could put that leash.

"Do you know why you're being punished, Andi?" he asked as he snapped the leash to the D ring.

She closed her eyes for a moment, then opened them to meet his gaze. "For disobeying you, Master. For climaxing without your permission."

He held the end of the leash in one hand and brushed his other knuckles across her cheek. She trembled beneath his touch. "You know I have to punish you. Remember that today."

Andi visibly swallowed. "Yes, Master."

He arranged her hair around her shoulders so that her breasts were clearly visible. "We're going to enjoy the amenities of the Club. I'll hold your leash, and you'll walk so that it's not too tight or too loose. You have to keep your eyes downcast. You can't look at anyone directly, unless I introduce you to them." He kept his tone intentionally stern and matter-of-fact. "When you're around another Dom, you have to keep your eyes down."

For a second he saw a glimmer of what looked like anger or frustration, but she bowed her head. "Yes, Master."

He hooked one finger under her chin and raised her face to look at him again. The glimmer was gone and her expression was resigned. "That's my baby." He brushed his lips over hers and she gave a sigh against his mouth. "Be a good girl and I won't have to punish you even more."

"Yes, Master," she whispered.

He gave her a wicked smile. "Good. Now let's eat breakfast."

Andi wasn't so sure what he had in mind, but she followed him to the table, the leash lightly pulling at her collar. Her ankles wobbled a bit in her stilettos, and she felt exposed and vulnerable in the skimpy clothing.

He seated himself at the lone chair before the table, which was situated so that it was somewhat sideways, facing her. He laid the leash across his lap, and gestured for her to kneel between his thighs. Andi held back a sigh as she knelt. *Here we go again.*

Only this time he immediately unfastened his leather pants and withdrew his erection. Andi's eyes widened.

He slipped his hand in her hair, forcing her forward so that her face was close to his cock. "I want you to suck me while I have my breakfast."

Andi's jaw dropped, and he took the opportunity to slide his length between her lips.

"That's it, baby." He kept one hand in her hair while he forced her head down as deep as she could take him.

At first she was too stunned to do anything, but when he said, "Andi . . ." in that warning tone, she started licking and sucking him in earnest. She used one hand to fondle his balls, while her other hand worked his cock. She found herself enjoying the feel of him in her mouth, the way his hardness slipped through her fingers, the taste of him on her tongue.

Derrick smiled as he took a sausage link in his free hand and bit into it. Damn, it felt good having Andi go down on him first thing in the morning. He held back his orgasm while he ate. She made small mewling sounds and hummed along his length, which brought him close to climax faster than he'd intended. He clenched his hand around his orange juice glass and watched his cock move in and out of Andi's mouth. It was too much.

His climax burst through him as his come spewed down her throat. He ground his teeth and the juice glass rattled on the table as he gripped it, fighting to keep from shouting out.

When the last of his semen spilled into her mouth, he took her leash and pulled on it, forcing her to stop. Andi looked up at him, licking the come from her lips. He released his grip on the juice glass and brushed Andi's hair from her eyes.

"Did you enjoy your breakfast, baby?" he asked.

Andi gave him a teasing smile. "Sausage is always good in the morning, Master."

Chapter 7

After feeding Andi scrambled eggs, sausage, and pancakes as she knelt before him, Derrick ordered her to stand. He tugged at her leash. "Now we'll go for a walk, baby."

Andi's cheeks burned as Derrick led her from the room into the hallway. God, she'd never been so embarrassed in all her life. As he led her by the leash, she wanted to fall through the floor every time they passed other Doms and subs. Few of the subs were on leashes like she was. She kept her gaze downcast as per Derrick's instructions, avoiding looking anyone in the eyes. That was one rule she was glad for. She'd die of embarrassment if she saw anyone at the resort who recognized her.

Of course, that would lead to the question of why *they* were here.

Cool air swept over her nearly naked body. With the G-string, her ass was completely exposed, the front barely covering the triangle of hair between her thighs. The bra felt sensuous as it rubbed against her nipples, and her breasts seemed on the verge of exploding from those little strips. Despite her nervousness, something about walking with practically nothing on past strangers was a little exciting. Her nipples stayed hard as jelly beans, and her juices dampened the leather strip of her G-string.

Derrick led her down the sweeping staircase to the large, elegant common room. His boots rang against the marble floor, and Andi's stilettos clicked with every step. From the corner of her eye, she saw appreciative glances from Doms and a few subs. One Dom outright leered at her and his stare made her skin crawl.

She kept her eyes lowered and avoided eye contact. Damned if she'd let anyone get to her.

They walked across the room, through the maze of lounge chairs and people chatting. Subs in various states of dress and undress stayed close to their Masters. Andi didn't feel quite so bad about her own near nakedness, considering what some of the women and men were wearing—or not wearing.

She followed Derrick through glass-and-mahogany doors and out into a beautiful paradise. Andi couldn't help but gaze in wonder beneath her lashes and sometimes peeking up. It was like what she would imagine a secret garden to be, with bowers of vines around and above them, intertwined with purple and pink flowers. A large fountain shot jets of water into the air that pattered like rain upon the pool surrounding it. Sunlight dappled the flagstones, and cushioned chairs crouched around tables throughout the arbor. Men and women lounged around the area, touching, kissing, and more. Much more.

As they worked their way through the arbor, Andi noticed private little corners where couples—or larger parties—could escape and enjoy some of the resort's amenities.

It was one such hideaway that Derrick led her into, with three leather-padded benches in a U shape. He slid onto one of the benches and patted his knee, indicating he wanted her to sit on his lap.

Andi's face still felt hot from their trek from the room to the arbor, and she was grateful to finally be someplace private with Derrick. Nothing in the boardroom, the office, or her life had prepared her for walking practically naked through crowds of people—on a frickin' leash, no less.

Derrick extended his arms. "Come here, baby."

"Yes, Master." Andi slid onto his lap. At first she was tense, but she relaxed against him. His butter-soft leather shirt and pants felt erotic against all her bare skin.

"Did you see how the other men and women looked at you?" He traced her lower lip with his index finger. "They wanted you, but you're all mine, and I'll do whatever I want to do with you."

Her voice came out low and husky as she replied, "Yes, Master."

"You look so damn hot." Derrick trailed his finger down to the hollow of her throat and then over one cup of the leather bra. "I want to taste what others can only dream of."

Derrick tugged on the cup and her breast sprang free, the nipple tightening in the cool air. He lowered his head and slipped his warm mouth over her taut nub, and she moaned at the exquisite feeling. While he suckled, he released her other breast, completely baring her. A part of her recognized that anyone could walk in on them, but right at that moment all that was important was his mouth and hands on her.

And when he slid one hand down her belly, she held her breath until he cupped her mound through the soft leather. He hooked one finger under the strip covering her folds and slipped the finger into her wetness. Andi cried out as he thrust inside her, his finger entering her channel the way she wanted his cock to plunge into her.

"Damn," he murmured as he raised his head. He brushed his lips over hers. "I love how wet you get. I can just imagine how good it's going to be when I fuck you. Once you've earned it."

God, she wanted him *now*.

"What—" She moaned again as he thrust three fingers into her this time. "What do I have to do, Master?"

His lips moved to her ear. "You have to obey my commands, follow protocol, do all I tell you to, and submit to me completely. Then you can have my cock inside you. I'll fuck you until you scream."

Andi shuddered from the combination of the erotic words, her breasts free in the cool air, and his fingers thrusting into her. Her climax was building, coming on like a storm.

"May I come, Master?" she asked while barely being able to breathe.

"No." He didn't let up on his strokes one bit. "Part of your training is to learn to withhold your own pleasure for mine." His lips brushed her earlobe, and his voice was barely a murmur. "Your job is to make sure I'm pleased. And right now it makes me hot to touch you like this."

God, she was simply going to explode if he kept teasing her. She fought to hold back her release, her muscles tense and perspiration coating her skin. When he finally eased his fingers from her pussy, she sagged against him in relief.

He brought his hand up to his mouth and sniffed. "Damn, you smell good, woman." He slipped his fingers into his mouth and tasted her juices. "And you taste," he said after he withdrew his fingers, "so good."

Andi shivered. She could smell her scent mixed with his masculine musk and the sweet fragrance of the flowers above and around them. They were in a paradise and it was only the two of them.

She stilled as she heard voices and the sound of footsteps. A gorgeous man and two women rounded the corner and entered the little hideaway. Andi's heart pounded and she tried to turn away and yank up her bra, but Derrick made her stop.

"Andi . . ." he said in that warning tone of his. "Do I need to punish you more?"

"No, Master," she muttered, keeping her eyes downcast and avoiding looking at the man and the women who'd reached them.

From the corner of her eye she saw the two women were on leashes, their eyes downcast, but without unhappy expressions on their pretty faces. Instead they looked appreciatively at Andi's breasts. The slaves wore matching metal-studded leather bustiers baring their tummies, skimpy panties, and thigh-high boots.

The man smiled, his eyes raking Andi's form as Derrick slid her from his lap and forced her to stand in front of the trio, before moving to her side.

"Derrick." The man reached out his hand and Derrick took it with a smile.

"Josh," he replied. "Just in time."

Andi's gaze shot up to look at Derrick. She quickly lowered her gaze again, her cheeks burning like wildfire.

Derrick turned his gaze on her. "Greet Master Josh, Andi."

She gave a bow from her shoulders. "My pleasure to meet you, Master Josh."

"Your slave is beautiful." He reached out and tweaked one of Andi's nipples, twisting it between his thumb and forefinger.

Andi gasped and stepped back, her gaze shooting up to meet his. "Stop!"

Derrick and the other Dom gave her looks that told her she had just made a very big mistake.

Andi's blood rushed in her ears.

The Dom twisted her nipple harder, then freed her as he looked to Derrick.

Andi lowered her gaze and Derrick sighed. "Apologize to Master Josh."

She wanted nothing more than to slap the crap out of both of them and knock the domineering looks right off their faces.

Instead she kept her eyes downcast and muttered, "My apologies, Master Josh."

"Of course, now she needs to be punished." Derrick focused his gaze on Master Josh.

Josh turned to his two slaves. "Flogger." One of the women handed him a braided flogger with strips of leather that looked much more menacing than what Derrick had used on her.

"Turn around," Master Josh said. "Place your hands on the back of the bench and show me your ass."

Andi trembled at the mere thought of the Dom whipping her. One look from Derrick and she knew she didn't have a choice.

Unless she wanted to shout out her safe word. Did she, though? Wasn't this part of her fantasy? Would this be the worst of it?

She slowly turned to face the bench, grabbed onto the back of it, and dug her nails into the padded backrest. Muscles throughout her body tensed as she waited for that first blow. Her breasts hung down, and the G-string presented her naked ass to the Dom.

She jerked when she felt a callused hand rub her buttocks, and she knew right away that it was Master Josh. She couldn't believe Derrick was letting another man touch her.

"You've got a gorgeous slave, Derrick," the man murmured, and she heard desire in his voice. "How about a trade? Lauren and Sara could both be yours for one night."

Andi's back went ramrod straight. He wouldn't dare!

"Maybe," Derrick said, and Andi almost screamed at him.

How dare he even consider trading her for a night with the subs? Giving her away?

But in the next moment the lash of the flogger tore all rational thought from her mind. Andi cried out at the harsh sting, and tears formed at the back of her eyes. She'd wanted this, fantasized about it, but reality was a different thing. Reality hurt.

"Not a sound," Derrick said in a warning tone.

There was a rustling noise and then Derrick moved a bright yellow ball before her gaze. "Bite this ball gag."

Andi hesitated only a second before sinking her teeth into the soft ball. A lash fell on her other ass cheek and she would have screamed again if it hadn't been for the ball gag in her mouth. The incredible sting of each lash fell with precision over her buttocks and thighs. To her surprise, the pain began to turn into a kind of pleasure. Amazingly, her pussy grew wet and her nipples tingled like her ass cheeks. And she was ready to come again!

The lashes stopped and she sagged in relief. She felt a hand caressing her buttocks, and this time she knew it was Derrick's touch.

He leaned close to her ear and murmured, "Very good, baby. Now behave and do what I ask you if you want to be in my bed and not Master Josh's."

He removed the ball from her mouth and took her by the arm, bringing her to a stand.

"Yes, Master." She was on the verge of either outright crying or climaxing, but she didn't want to give the safe word. She wanted to go through with this, but if he tried to give her away . . .

What's wrong with me? I thought I'd be here with a stranger, after all. It might be easier with someone I don't know. Hell. Master Josh might even fuck me and give me some relief!

But the thought of being with Master Josh really, really bothered her. She felt a new coolness toward Derrick. This was just a game to him. A conquest. She'd need to keep that in mind.

She added, "I won't disappoint you, Master."

"That's my girl." Derrick turned her to face the Dom and his subs, and she kept her eyes lowered. "Now sit between Lauren and Sara."

The subs stepped forward and took Andi by her arms, positioning her between them on the middle bench. The subs were pretty, both with dark brown hair—they were twins, Andi realized. Every man's dream.

Derrick and Master Josh sat on the benches to either side of the women, across from each other.

"Look at me, Andi," Derrick said. She raised her eyes and met his. "I'd really like to see Lauren and Sara touch you."

Chapter 8

Andi's eyes widened and she dropped her jaw. *You want what?* she almost shouted.

"Relax, baby." Derrick's beautiful blue eyes had a calming effect, like the ocean. "You need to learn to enjoy your body with no shame, no reservations."

Andi took a deep breath. She could do this. She wouldn't let him have the opportunity to punish her again. "Yes . . . Master."

Josh leaned back on his bench with his arms folded across his large chest and a very obvious bulge in his black pants. He had silver chains draping his pants and vest. Like Derrick, he was a powerful and good-looking man, but with blond hair and gray eyes. "You can talk if you want," he said to his subs.

"Thank you, Master," Sara said with a smile lighting her pretty features. She raised her hand and stroked Andi's hair from where it had fallen across one breast. "She is a beautiful slave."

Andi wanted to scream *I'm not a slave*, but instead she found herself quivering at Sara's touch.

"She has a perfect figure." Lauren traced her fingers along the inside of Andi's thigh and, despite herself, Andi's thong grew very damp.

Andi's gaze met Derrick's as the women caressed her, and she saw such fierce desire in his eyes that she felt even more turned on. Even the stinging on her ass added to her pleasure.

But when Sara's mouth latched onto Andi's nipple, she almost shouted in surprise. Before she had time to fully register what was happening, Lauren had begun suckling her other nipple, and Andi did cry out this time at the incredible sensations rippling through her body.

Her gaze shot to Derrick and he smiled. "Relax, baby. Enjoy. Your pleasure gives me pleasure."

Andi gave herself up to the sensations of the women stroking her, licking and lightly biting her nipples. When they both slid their fingers beneath the strip of cloth covering her mound, Andi thought she'd come unglued from both embarrassment and pleasure. Lauren and Sara stroked and fondled her, bringing her higher and higher toward that peak, and she didn't know if she could hold back much longer. Her gaze locked with Derrick's and he slowly shook his head *no*.

Oh, God, he was trying to kill her.

In the next moment Sara's mouth met hers, and she slipped her tongue between Andi's lips. At first she was too shocked to move, but then she gave herself up to the kiss. Sara's mouth was softer than a man's, her taste different—sweeter somehow. Even the gentleness of her tongue was different than a man's. In the meantime, Lauren ran her tongue along the collar around Andi's neck, causing her to shiver.

Andi heard a soft purring sound, and realized it was coming from her. She was *enjoying* this. She had never fantasized about women, and here she was making out with *two* women, in front of two men.

God, it was hot.

Lauren slipped her hand from Andi's folds, then caught Andi's chin in her hand. "My turn." She pulled her away from Sara's kiss and locked her lips to Andi's. Lauren's kiss was fiercer, more intense, and Andi grew more aroused than ever. Lauren tasted different than Sara—of peppermint and iced tea.

Sara's fingers still stroked Andi's clit and she continued to suckle one of Andi's nipples. Between Lauren's kiss and Sara's touch, Andi was growing wilder by the minute. She slipped away from the real world, their bodies entwining on the bench and their hands everywhere as each one took turns kissing her. Lauren took one of Andi's hands, guiding it to her own pussy and pulling aside the material of the spandex suit she wore.

Shock rippled through Andi at feeling another woman's folds, to feel the slick flesh beneath her fingers. Tentatively Andi began stroking Lauren's clit, then her touch became stronger the louder Lauren's moans became.

Sara guided Andi's hand to her pussy, and Andi found herself stroking two women at once.

Lauren gasped and said, "May I come, Master?"

"You and Sara both may climax," he replied.

Andi broke her kiss with Sara, and her gaze went to Derrick. He shook his head. "No. You can't, Andi."

She almost screamed her frustration and anger at the same moment both Lauren and Sara were shouting out as their hips bucked against Andi's hands.

Andi squirmed, fighting her own orgasm. *Damn it*, she wouldn't come without Derrick's permission. She wouldn't disappoint him in front of another Master and his subs. She had once, but she wouldn't do it again. *Damn*, it pissed her off.

As she slipped her fingers from their folds, the women removed their hands and mouths from Andi, and cuddled against her for a moment. Andi's body still throbbed and she was so sexually frustrated that she could barely think clearly.

She glanced from Derrick to Master Josh and saw the satisfied but almost pained expressions on both their faces.

"Master Josh needs relief." Derrick gestured toward the Dom. "Use that perfect mouth on him, Andi. Then let him come all over your beautiful breasts."

Andi gaped at him. He was going to make her suck another man's cock?

Derrick raised an eyebrow and Andi knew it was her choice. She could say her safe word now, and the weekend would end, or she could go down on Master Josh.

When her gaze locked with Derrick's, she saw how much the thought of watching her suck another man's cock turned him on. Would he want another man to fuck her, though?

It wasn't like they meant anything to each other—just a weekend of sex, and then it was back to the real world. A conquest. A game. Yes, definitely, that's all it was.

Andi's pussy started to throb as she realized that she was really going to suck a man's cock in front of Derrick. And the fact had her body on fire with excitement.

Andi pulled away from the two women and approached the other Dom. "What would you like me to do, Master Josh?"

"On your knees, slave."

Andi tensed at the word *slave*, but she obeyed, and kept her eyes fixed on the bulge in his crotch, avoiding his gaze as she knelt.

While she watched, he stood in front of her, unfastened his pants, and pulled out his erection. It was almost as long as Derrick's, and thicker, with a darker, plum-colored head. He fisted his erection, running his hand along the length of it.

The man was handsome enough to make a woman's heart stop, and his voice was deep and throbbing. "If I'm not happy with the way you suck me off, I'm sure Master Derrick will punish you again."

"Yes, Master Josh," she said. Her body quaked. God, she was really going to do this. And she was excited about it.

He released his cock and thrust his hips forward. Andi lowered her head and flicked her tongue over the tip. A bead of come was in the tiny slit and she tasted him, finding a somewhat different flavor than Derrick's. She was positioned in such a way that she could see Derrick from beneath her lashes. The twins had moved to sit on either side of Derrick. They had removed their bustiers so that they were naked from the waist up, and only wore their skimpy panties and boots. Derrick had his arms around both of them and lightly stroked their shoulders as he watched Andi lave her tongue along Master Josh's erection. A spurt of jealousy surged through her at the sight of Derrick touching the other women.

As she licked Josh's cock she thought she saw a flicker of jealousy in Derrick's blue eyes. Master Josh took her face in his palms and forced her to look up at him. "I want you to watch me while I fuck your mouth."

Andi obeyed, keeping her gaze focused on Master Josh's gray eyes, and a strange feeling tingled through her belly. He began thrusting his hips forward, in and out of her mouth as she flicked her tongue along his length. She brought her hands up and began fondling his balls with one hand while wrapping the fingers of her other around his erection, working him in time with his thrusts.

She couldn't believe how wet this was making her, how hard her nipples were. And what surprised her most was that her increased arousal was purely because she knew Derrick was watching—and she knew it was causing incredible sexual tension within him.

"That's it, slave," Josh said in a rumbling voice. "Suck harder."

Still watching the Dom, Andi increased the pressure of her tongue and her hands, and sucked *hard*.

Master Josh shouted and pulled his cock from her mouth. He fisted his length and pointed his cock at her chest. Come spurted out in jets over her neck and her naked breasts. The streams of semen were warm, but quickly cooled against her skin.

When the last drop had spilled from his cock, Master Josh gestured to Lauren and Sara. In a rumbling voice, still filled with passion, he said to the twins, "Clean Andi—with your tongues."

"Yes, Master," they said in unison.

Andi bit the inside of her lip as the two women came over, got down on their hands and knees, and began licking the come from her breasts and neck.

Andi tilted her head back and allowed herself to enjoy the feel of their tongues and lips. She glanced at Derrick and saw approval in his eyes, and his erection looked even bigger, if that was possible.

When the women had finished licking every drop of come from Andi's chest and neck, Master Josh drew her to her feet and sat on the bench, and brought her onto his lap. His still-naked cock was erect again, and it dug into the crack of her ass cheeks. She clenched her fists, praying Derrick wasn't going to tell Master Josh that it was okay to fuck her.

"Now," Master Josh said, "it's time for Lauren and Sara to pleasure Master Derrick."

At Andi's startled look of jealousy, Derrick smiled. *Good.* She didn't like the idea of other women having him.

She quickly hid her emotions by giving him a look of indifference, but he knew she was anything but indifferent.

Derrick settled back against the bench and let the twins unzip his leather pants down past his balls to free his incredible erection. Watching the twins all over Andi, then seeing her bring Josh to climax, followed by the twins licking Josh's come off of her, had turned him on to the point that his cock had threatened to burst the seams of his pants.

As Sara slipped her mouth over Derrick's cock, Lauren began sucking his balls, drawing them one at a time into her mouth and applying light suction. The pressure she applied gave him a small burst of pain that enhanced his pleasure.

What made him even hotter was seeing the jealousy in Andi's eyes as she sat in Josh's lap. The Dom lightly stroked her nipples while she watched the twins suck Derrick off, and he could tell she was so on edge from her need to climax that she was ready to scream.

It turned him on, too, to know that Josh's naked cock was pressed against Andi's bare ass, as if ready to take her there. Derrick wouldn't allow Josh to fuck Andi's pussy, but there was a good chance that Josh would be thrusting into Andi's ass at the same time Derrick was deep inside her slick core.

Even though Andi might not realize it yet, Derrick knew she would experience pleasure like she'd never had before, with two men, and that thought alone just about made him come.

He focused on the feel of the twins licking and sucking his cock but still watched Andi. Her nipples were taut, and Josh was moving her back and forth on his lap, rubbing his cock along her crack. He imagined that, instead of the twins going down on him, he was driving his cock deep within Andi's slick core.

Derrick came with a rumble that rose out of his throat in a

near growl. He jerked his cock from Sara's mouth. He spurted onto Lauren and Sara's faces and chests as they continued to milk his come from his body.

Josh squeezed Andi's waist and moved his lips near her ear. "Clean up the girls," he ordered. "Using your tongue."

Chapter 9

A breeze rustled the leaves and flowers around them, while everyone waited for Andi to obey. She swallowed past a sudden burst of shyness at the thought of having her tongue on the women. It was one thing to have their hands and mouths on her, another to be the one sucking and licking.

Master Josh slipped her off his lap, forcing her to stand. His cock slid across her bare skin and she couldn't help but imagine what it would be like to be with Derrick and Master Josh at the same time.

"Clean up the girls, slave," he repeated, with a harder edge to his words, and she knew he wasn't happy that she hadn't answered yet. She certainly didn't want that flogger on her ass again.

"Yes, Master Josh." She wobbled across the flagstone to the twins in her heels, heat filling her as she thought about what she was about to do.

Derrick instructed the twins to sit on the bench, and Andi

knelt between Sara's thighs. The flagstone was hard against her knees, but Sara's thighs were soft around her waist.

Hesitantly, Andi leaned forward and flicked her tongue along a stream of come that was rolling down Sara's breast. The sub sighed and gripped Andi's hair in her hands.

Andi licked harder, with more purpose, and was amazed at how much she liked the taste of Derrick's come mixed with the salt of Sara's skin. Nervousness spiraled in Andi's belly as she licked one path of come down to the woman's nipple. Purely out of curiosity, she sucked the sub's nipple, drawing it into her mouth and lightly biting it. Sara moaned and thrust her breast farther into Andi's mouth. Sara smelled of come, the musk from between her thighs, and a light citrus fragrance.

Andi found the feel of the nipple unusual in her mouth. Soft, yet hard, and the areola was puckered and bumpy to her tongue. Hardly conscious of anyone else, Andi moved her mouth to Sara's other nipple and sucked it despite the fact that there wasn't any come on it. After nipping at Sara, Andi finished licking the rest of Derrick's semen from the woman's body. He had even come on Sara's face, and Andi licked it away, too. When she flicked a drop from the corner of Sara's mouth, the woman let out a soft sigh and turned her lips to Andi's. They kissed, a long and sweet kiss that made Andi's heart race.

"Lauren is waiting," came Derrick's voice, gruff and deep as if aroused beyond normal speech.

Andi broke the kiss, barely holding back a smile. She hoped Derrick's cock was so hard it was ready to burst through his pants.

She was certainly too hot for words. Actually licking and kissing women, going down on another man in front of her "Master," and being kissed and fondled by strange men and women, was unbelievably erotic. She'd never dreamed she'd be doing anything like this, or how much she'd enjoy it.

She left Sara to kneel between Lauren's legs. The beautiful woman spread her thighs wide, and Andi smelled her musk. Before she had a chance to catch her breath, Lauren kissed her hard and fast. Andi sighed at the feel of the kiss, then moved her mouth away, licking at the drying come on Lauren's cheek. The sub pinched and pulled Andi's nipples while she flicked her tongue along the trails of come, going over Lauren's collar, her neck, and down to her breasts.

"That's it, baby." Derrick's voice was even huskier. "Clean her off."

Andi moved farther down, and Lauren eased her hands into Andi's hair. Andi enjoyed paying attention to the woman's nipples the same way she had sucked Sara's.

When she finished, she sat back on her haunches, her hands in her lap, and looked up at Derrick. "What do you want me to do now, Master?" she asked, hoping he would let her come.

He stroked a strand of hair from her face and tucked it behind her ear. "It's time for lunch."

Andi was mortified. She sat at the luncheon table with Derrick, her entire body burning with embarrassment as he forced her to eat lunch with her bra still under her breasts. Her nipples betrayed her, puckering to hard, taut peaks, and her folds dampened with more moisture.

Damn it, how could he make her do this? Yet somehow it turned her on.

One consolation was that many of the women and men seated

at other tables were as bared as she was, if not more so. Around them were other couples, threesomes, and even larger groups. Open displays of sexuality were obviously the norm, as were nakedness and near nakedness. Hell, once Andi's mortification lessened, she allowed herself to glance around and saw slaves of both genders who were completely naked. Many were on leashes, too.

Yet she still found her hands easing up to her breasts, wanting to cup them, hide them.

"Stop." Derrick placed his hand over hers and met her eyes. Electricity zinged through her at his touch. "Be proud. Display those beautiful breasts." His eyes narrowed with what appeared to be lust. "Right now I want to take you to our room, spank your ass, and fuck you until you can't walk."

Andi gulped. His words, the huskiness in his voice, the way he looked at her, all made her so hot she could barely stand it. Since she hadn't been allowed to have an orgasm today, she was so raw and horny that she was sure she could come with just a rub of her thong against her clit.

No. She wouldn't succumb. She wouldn't give Derrick the satisfaction of it, allowing him to punish her in Lord knew what way he would come up with.

They were seated at a table in a beautiful courtyard surrounded by lush vegetation and a variety of colorful flowers. Afternoon sunshine warmed all her bared skin, and the air smelled good, of grilled chicken, fresh-baked rolls, and roasted meats. The additional scent of flowers and fresh air relaxed her. A little.

The waiter brought the meal Derrick had ordered, and Andi avoided his eyes. When she reached for her glass of Chardonnay, she felt the weight of the leash tug against her neck, and the soft leather collar seemed a little more constricting than it had before. Maybe it was the fact that she was having a hard time swallowing down her lust for Derrick.

Over the rim of her wineglass she studied him, admiring his profile as he said something to the waiter. Derrick's features were strong and masculine, and she liked the way he focused on whatever task was before him, whether it was in the boardroom, or here at the resort, dominating her.

She carefully set the wineglass back on the table. Just the thought of what he might have in mind for her threw her off balance. *Jeez*, she told herself, *you're a Vice President of a major corporation, for Christ's sake.* She was confident, self-assured, in control of herself and her environment.

So why did she feel the opposite around Derrick—like she could just let him take care of her, and do anything he commanded her to do?

When the waiter left, Derrick said, "Eat your lunch before I devour you in front of everyone." Those incredible blue eyes burned through her, telling her he meant what he said.

"Yes, Master." She slowly ate her Atlantic salmon, bathed in capers and lemon butter. The broccoli, carrots, and yellow squash were crisp, the way she liked them, and the side of wild rice was cooked to perfection.

"That's my girl," Derrick said, and she was certain she heard humor in his voice. No doubt from the way she was devouring her meal. After all that sex—well, almost-sex on her part—she was ravenous.

When she had eaten her last bite of salmon, she glanced up to see Derrick watching her. His empty plate was pushed away from him, his arms folded on the tabletop, and he gazed at her intently. Andi's head swam, and she couldn't help but wonder if it was the wine or the way Derrick affected her.

"Lean closer." He reached for his glass of Chardonnay, and held it near his lips. His breath fogged the glass.

Andi's belly fluttered as she obeyed, feeling his heat against her.

Derrick sipped his wine, then set the glass on the table. He slipped his fingers into her hair and brought his lips to hers.

Andi opened for him, expecting the thrust of his tongue. Instead he fed her the wine from his mouth. Her world spun. The wine was so much more intoxicating coming from him, as the warmth of the fluid slid over her tongue and down her throat.

She melted so completely against him that she lost track of herself and everything around them. He placed his hand against the small of her back, crushing her harder to him, smashing her breasts against his butter-soft leather shirt.

The last of the wine passed from his mouth to hers and his tongue replaced it, delving into her warmth as if to explore every bit of her. She clenched her fists in his shirt, her tongue meeting his. He tasted of wine and pure male, and he smelled of the clean scent of soap and musky aftershave.

She clung tighter to him, not wanting to break the kiss, not wanting to lose the precious contact between them.

Derrick pulled away and her breath came in hard, hungry gasps. Her body trembled with need, for whatever he would give her, and her mind could hardly wrap around the unbelievable desire she felt for the man.

His eyes caught her, held her. "Your turn," he murmured in a husky voice that told her he was just as hot as she was.

For a moment she didn't know what he meant, but when he glanced at her Chardonnay she reached for it. Her fingers barely held on to the glass as she brought it to her lips, and she felt a little of it dribble onto her chin as she took a mouthful of the wine and held it, not swallowing.

When she set the glass down, Derrick leaned close again. Instead of meeting her lips, he flicked his tongue out, tasting the drops of wine on her chin.

He slowly moved his lips to hers and opened his mouth. She fed him the wine, letting it trickle from her lips onto his tongue.

Derrick groaned and smashed their lips together, and clenched his hand so tight in her hair that the pain of it startled her, yet it quickly melded into a pleasure that joined the incredible kiss.

When he slipped his tongue from her mouth and raised his head to look into her eyes, he slid one hand from her hair to cup the side of her face. Andi leaned into his palm, feeling almost as if her muscles and limbs would no longer support her.

He touched the tip of her nose with one finger and gave her a sensual smile. "Did you know I've wanted to kiss you since the first moment I saw you?"

Andi's heart beat a little faster. "I thought you barely knew I existed, Master."

"How could I not notice you? You strode into the office with such confidence and grace you stole my breath away." He smiled as he traced his finger down her nose. "And now you're mine."

Her head briefly swam with his words, but she reminded herself how easily he had given her to another man. "For this weekend, yes . . . Master."

He just smiled. "Come on. I'll show you around."

Andi took a shaky breath and nodded. She didn't know what had just happened, but whatever it was, it scared the hell out of her. Even more than all the bondage and punishments he'd come up with so far.

Chapter 10

Derrick and Andi walked hand in hand around the lush re-sort. He held the leash, too, but needed the warmth of her small hand in his.

He couldn't get enough of her. He knew he never would. He enjoyed everything about her: the way she didn't back down in the boardroom when she felt strongly about an issue; the way she was willing to compromise; the way she treated her employees with fairness, yet with the firmness of a good manager.

From watching her all this time, he knew she was a good and loyal friend, and she would do anything for hers. She was honest and forthcoming—you always knew where you stood with Andi.

And damn, but she was beautiful. Her gorgeous breasts, her long black hair, her soft curves, and long legs . . . God, he wanted to fuck her. It took a tight rein on his control to keep himself from taking her down to the grass and thrusting his cock into her slick warmth now, in front of everyone in the damn resort.

No. He would wait until they were alone like he had planned, and then he would have her.

He had always enjoyed watching his women being pleasured by other men and women in the past. Today, though, had been difficult. No matter how much it had turned him on, he'd wanted to whisk Andi away and keep her all to himself.

Yet he was looking forward to tonight, in the dungeon. He couldn't wait to see her face while she was pleasured as she'd never been pleasured before.

But first he had to have her. Alone.

His steps became more urgent as they neared one of the themed cabanas, and he had to force himself to slow down. Andi tottered on her heels as she walked over the uneven lawn, and he liked it when she lost her balance and her nearly naked body brushed his.

When they reached an elegant tent, Derrick pushed the door flap open and watched Andi's face as she took in the surroundings.

It was absolutely decadent, Andi thought as she gazed around the enormous room. It looked like a sultan's harem tent might look, filled with embroidered brocade pillows that covered every inch of the floor and exquisite tapestries that hung along the walls. It smelled of exotic spices and light sandalwood incense. A tall golden pole at the center of the tent supported the ceiling, which rose far above their heads.

Against one wall of the tent she also saw what looked like two changing rooms. Next to them was a collection of whips, scarves, and floggers of different colors and sizes hanging from the dressing room wall. Andi bit her lower lip, wondering what Derrick had in mind. He was always surprising her.

She glanced up and met his blue eyes, and saw a wicked gleam mixed with lust.

"Get in here," he said. He tugged her hand and she stumbled over a pillow, barely keeping her balance as he led her to the changing room. He pulled aside a drape and she saw a golden costume that looked like a harem outfit. He slipped the garments from the hanger and handed the top and bottom to her. "Put these on."

She clutched it to her chest, the silky material sensitizing her taut nipples. "Yes, Master."

"Leave off your thong, and your heels, too." Derrick gripped her chin and trailed his thumb over her lips. "And don't make me wait."

Andi shivered from his touch. "Yes, Master," she said as he left, letting the drape fall shut behind him.

She turned and caught a movement out of the corner of her eye, seeing her reflection in a mirror that hung on one side of the dressing room. For one long moment she stared at herself, her eyes dark with arousal.

Her long dark hair hung over her shoulders, looking tousled and windblown, and her naked breasts were lifted up, with the bra pulled down beneath them. Her nipples were taut and her skin was flushed. She looked like a woman who desperately needed to be fucked.

With a start she remembered Derrick's command to not keep him waiting. She stripped out of her thong, her bra, and her heels, and slipped on the silk top with its sheer sleeves. The top didn't fasten, and with every move she made it fell open to reveal her breasts. The pants' waistband was silk, but the legs were sheer, and she could see the curls at the apex of her thighs.

And they were crotchless.

A thrill skittered through Andi's belly, and she hoped this meant Derrick would finally fuck her.

"Andi . . ." came his voice from outside the changing room with a note of warning in his tone. She pulled aside the drape and stepped barefoot upon one of the velvety pillows on the tent's floor.

Derrick's eyes flared and his jaw tightened, as if he was reining himself in. He looked absolutely gorgeous and her arousal deepened as she took him in. The muscles in his biceps flexed as he folded his arms across his well-built chest. His waist tapered down to trim hips and gold silk sultan's pants covered his long legs. His erection was a huge bulge against the silk.

She took a deep breath and put her hands behind her back, widened her stance, and lowered her gaze, hoping he wouldn't punish her for lack of protocol.

"Good," he murmured, and she shivered at his husky tone. "Come to me."

Andi obeyed, keeping her eyes downcast. The velvet and brocade pillows were both soft and coarse in texture beneath her bare feet, and she had to watch where she stepped to avoid tripping.

"On your knees, baby," he said in a voice hoarse with desire when she reached him.

Andi obeyed, feeling the softness of the pillows beneath her knees when she knelt. She watched as he rubbed his erection through his silk harem pants, then freed his cock through an opening that she hadn't noticed before.

He slipped his hand into her hair and guided her forward so

that her lips were a hairbreadth away from his erection. A drop of semen glistened in the low lighting, and she licked her lips.

"Suck me, my little harem girl," he said in a formal, imperious voice like he really was a sultan. He clenched her hair tighter, "I'll reward you well if you perform to my liking."

Her belly twisted with excitement and she started to reach up with one hand when he stopped her. "Use only your mouth," he said.

"Yes, Master." She crossed her hands behind her back, hoping he'd be happy enough to take her *finally*.

With his hand still clenched in her hair, he pushed his cock through her lips as he thrust forward. Andi took him deep, feeling him at the back of her throat. She licked and sucked and found herself moaning as he fucked her mouth.

"That's it, baby." He groaned as he thrust harder yet, and the silk of his sultan's pants brushed her face as he ground his hips against her. "Now look at me."

Andi's gaze met his as he watched his cock move in and out of her mouth. Her breasts bounced beneath her gold silk harem top, and the silk rubbed her nipples until she thought she'd scream from the sensation. Her sex ached and the material of her harem pants dampened. She wanted to slip her fingers into her folds to bring herself to what she knew would be a shattering orgasm.

Derrick groaned and she felt his cock tighten in her mouth. Just as she thought he was going to come, he pulled her head back and withdrew his erection.

She watched as he closed his eyes for a moment and tilted his head back. She knew he was struggling to gain control and a rush of satisfaction traveled through her because he had to fight so hard to keep from coming.

His voice was a low rumble when he released her hair to gesture at the tent pole. "Lie flat on your back, your arms above your head and to either side of the pole."

"Yes, Master." Shivers ran up and down Andi's spine as she settled against the pillows and raised her arms up. The harem top fell open and she almost grinned when Derrick gave a low groan, his gaze fixed on her naked breasts.

"Don't move," he ordered as he turned and moved to the wall of objects she had noticed earlier. When he returned he was carrying a gold silk scarf in one hand and his other fist was clenched around something she couldn't see.

He moved behind the pole where he was out of her sight, then took her wrists in his hands. He tied her to the pole, the bindings snug against her wrists.

When he returned to her, he knelt between her thighs, nudging them farther apart so that she was splayed wide open. She felt the rush of cold air against her wet folds through the crotchless pants.

Derrick opened his hand and she saw two clamps with golden beads dangling from them. She caught her breath as he raised one to her nipple and clamped it onto the hardened nub.

The instant pain caused her to gasp, but then she was arching her back at the pleasure of it, her body begging for more. He smiled and clamped the other one to her bare nipple, and she bit her lip to keep from moaning. The clamps felt tight, like Derrick was biting her nipples, and the dangling beads lightly caressed the swell of her breasts. The pleasure and pain were incredibly erotic, and she was even more turned on than she had been before, which was definitely saying something.

"You're so beautiful, baby." He cupped her breasts and massaged them, and she felt like blood was rushing straight to her head. "I can't wait to fuck you."

"Yes, Master." Andi raised her hips in a plea for him to take her. "*Yes.*"

Derrick groaned and grasped his cock in his hand. He brought the head to her folds, and rubbed it against her slick flesh. She pulled against her bonds, wanting to reach for him, at the same time she squirmed with the need to have him deep inside her.

He stroked her clit with the head of his cock while he kept his gaze focused on hers. "Are you ready to be fucked?"

Andi almost screamed. "Yes, Master. Please fuck me. Fuck me as hard as you can."

Derrick gave her a look of satisfaction the moment before he drove his cock inside her.

This time she did scream. It came out of nowhere, shocking her the same way her body was shocked at how he filled her and stretched her wide. She pumped her hips in rhythm with him. She tugged against her silken bonds, wanting to go wild beneath him. Wanting to scrape her nails along his back, down to his tight ass, where she would clench him as he drove in and out of her.

He fucked her so hard her head banged against the pole and his hips bruised the insides of her thighs. The tent seemed to swirl around her, the bright colors blending with the incredible sensations she was experiencing. The clamps tight upon her nipples, the silk and gauze of the harem outfit against her skin. The feel of every thrust Derrick made within her.

She was so close to coming, so close. Vaguely she remembered she wasn't supposed to come without permission and she barely kept from toppling over the edge before she asked him, "Please may I come, Master?"

"Not yet." Sweat rolled down his strong jaw and his dark hair was damp around her face. His arms were braced to either side of her head and his biceps bulged.

Andi moaned, so close to coming that she was certain she wouldn't make it a moment longer. And then he shouted, "Come for me, baby!" and her world spun out of control as she screamed. Her climax hit her so powerfully that her body bucked with one aftershock after another.

Derrick shouted again and she felt his cock pumping within her core, his warmth filling her up.

He collapsed against her, just holding himself up enough so that he wasn't crushing her. "My God, Andi." His breathing came sharp and fast. "What have you done to me?"

She was breathing so hard she couldn't have gotten a word out if she'd tried. Spasms continued to rock her body, her pussy clenching around Derrick's cock, still buried inside her.

He gave a low groan and brushed his lips over hers. "You're mine, baby. All mine."

Chapter 11

After another erotic meal, a dinner that had left her beyond needing a climax again, Derrick led Andi by her leash to the dungeon. She wore only the G-string now, and her high heels. He had also insisted on protocol this time, and she walked with her eyes downcast, her hands behind her back, several paces behind him.

And her heart was pounding like mad.

Her heels clicked against stone as he led her down spiraling steps into the dark depths beneath the resort. Down, down, down.

The world slipped away when the steps ended at a darkened corridor that was a tunnel carved in stone. She became aware of the hiss and spit of torches burning in brackets, the only light offered in the dimness. There was only the sound of her breathing, the feeling of cool air against her naked breasts, and the dank smell of the tunnel, the clunk of Derrick's boots, and the steady drop of water in the distance.

Andi shivered and slowed as a moment of fear overcame her. *What am I doing?*

A tug on her leash brought her back to the moment, and Derrick narrowed his eyes as he glanced at her over his shoulder. "Do you need more punishments, baby?"

"No, Master." Andi lowered her eyes again and increased her pace to keep up with his. She had to remind herself that this was what she came here for. She *wanted* this. *Wanted* to turn over control. *Wanted* to pleasure and be pleasured in every way imaginable.

And she had experienced things today that topped the pleasure charts.

When they entered another corridor, it was exactly as she had pictured it. Very medieval, almost frightening. Wooden door after wooden door ran the length of the corridor. At each door was a small barred window. Some were closed, but others remained open—perhaps closed for privacy, or open so that voyeurs were free to watch.

She swallowed down another gulp of fear as sounds of screams, shouts, and soft cries met her ears. Chains rattled, whips smacked flesh, and orders were shouted with answering cries of "Yes, Master!" or "Yes, Sire!"

"Shit," Andi muttered without thinking.

Derrick came to an abrupt stop and she smacked into him, feeling all that hard male flesh against her naked breasts, and the heat of him radiating through her body like a branding iron.

"You've broken another rule," he said, turning to her, his face as serious as if she had committed the worst of crimes. "You're not allowed to speak unless I say you can."

She tipped her chin up a notch, and raised her voice. "Yes, Master." Then she realized her mistake and lowered her gaze, but still looked at him from beneath her lashes.

No smile from him, only complete seriousness. "Another punishment, baby. Better make sure you don't break any more rules."

Shit, Andi thought, this time keeping it to herself as Derrick turned and tugged at her leash.

At the very end of the corridor, Derrick paused in front of a huge, rough-hewn wooden door. This one had a larger window opening, with thick iron bars. She waited with her heart in her throat as he tugged at the door. It creaked open, echoing eerily down the corridor.

He stepped into the dungeon room and pulled her leash, making her follow. When she entered the room she came to a dead stop. Her skin flushed with heat and she grew light-headed.

Master Josh stood nude in the center of the enormous room, whip in hand, his gaze centered on Andi. In those few seconds of recognition, she saw that Sara was naked, on her knees in a cage, her wrists bound to one of the bars over her head. Lauren was spread-eagle, her arms and wrists tied to the wooden arms of a St. Andrew's cross, and she was just as bare as everyone else.

Andi's first instinct was to turn and run. Derrick had something planned for her, and she wasn't sure she was going to like it. At all.

Derrick tugged at her leash again, and she turned her wide gaze on him. There he was, looking as incredibly handsome and dangerous as ever. Just how dangerous could he be?

He came up close to her so that she again felt his heat, and despite herself she wanted to melt into him. He reached up and unsnapped the leash from her collar. "Safe, sane, and consensual, baby." He let the catch on the leash trail down her shoulder. "Anything you can't handle, just say your safe word and this all ends."

At that moment, with him so close and making her dizzy with

lust, she wasn't sure she could remember her safe word. *France? Italy? No, Monaco, that was it.*

She hoped.

"Yes, Master," she said, and he smiled.

"That's my girl." His face again became a mask of dominance as he turned to Master Josh.

"Is the slave ready?" Master Josh asked as he lightly snapped his whip.

Andi gulped.

Derrick gave a slow nod and glanced toward a pair of handcuffs dangling from a long, thick-linked chain. Andi's gaze traveled up the chain to see that it was attached to an iron ring secured in the stone ceiling of the dungeon.

"Stand beneath the handcuffs," Derrick commanded. "For your first punishment you'll accept whatever Master Josh and I want to do to you."

She sucked in her breath as she walked past Sara's cage and tried not to look at Lauren's naked form across the room, where the woman was strapped to the St. Andrew's cross. Andi couldn't help but peek from the corner of her eye. Lauren's head was tilted to the side, her eyes at half-mast, and she looked as if she was in another world altogether.

When Andi stood beneath the chain, Master Josh took one of her arms while Derrick took the other, and they fastened her wrists into the cuffs. Master Josh's cock brushed her thigh, and heat rose within Andi at the contact.

The metal cuffs were fur-lined, thank God. She dangled from the chain, the toes of her stilettos barely scraping the dungeon's stone floor. She felt strung out and light-headed, her arms high over her head, and her body extending down as if she were being stretched like human taffy.

Derrick started to strip, pulling his soft leather shirt over his head and tossing it aside. His muscles flexed, his nipples hard, and the bulge beneath his leather pants told her how turned on he was.

Andi took a second to take in a huge room that could have been from King Arthur's time. The walls were made of stone, crumbling in some places. The floor was probably hewn from handmade blocks. But even though the setting looked authentic, it still appeared to be clean—as if all was kept sterile.

Her gaze tried to take in everything else in the room. Floggers, whips, chains, and other medieval-like torture devices lined the wall across from her. Some of the warmth left her body. She didn't *even want* to know what some of them were.

To her right was a stockade next to a table with leather straps and metal stirrups. There was a leather swing in one corner, and a leather-covered sawhorse to her left. Her skin grew colder with every new discovery.

What *was* that damn safe word again? *Monaco. Yeah, that's it.*

Master Josh left Andi's side to go to Lauren. He snapped his whip and it smacked against the woman's thigh. Her eyes flew open and she gave a small cry.

"Your punishment is to watch while slave Andi is pleasured." His tone was firm and his eyes intent as he glanced Andi's way. Wildfire flared within her belly and heat flowed over her at his words. What was going to happen? Were they all going to watch as Derrick fucked her? The mere thought was heady, arousing, and confusing all at once.

Master Josh turned his gaze back to Lauren. "You've got to learn you're not allowed to climax without my permission with anyone but me, as long as you are my slave."

Lauren nodded and visibly swallowed. "Yes, Master. I'll never do it again."

Josh moved to Sara's cage. He snapped the whip and she jerked against her bonds. "Your punishment is the same, slave," he said. "You and your sister were bad today, weren't you." A statement, not a question.

Sara licked her lips. "Yes, Master."

Master Josh gave one quick nod, the fierce expression still on his strikingly handsome features. He moved back toward Andi, and her gaze flicked toward Derrick. . . .

Who was now completely and gloriously naked. Her heart pounded faster and her mouth grew dry as her gaze rested on his erect cock, rising from its nest of soft, dark curls. His balls were large, and she imagined herself taking each one in her mouth and sucking before going down on his cock.

God, how she wanted him to fuck her again.

But then Master Josh pressed his cock against her thigh and stroked the leather strap of the whip over her breasts, scraping her nipples. She gasped. She tore her gaze from Derrick to Josh, her lips parting in surprise.

Master Josh dove for her mouth, his tongue slipping into her depths before she had a chance to realize what was happening. The way he teased her with his tongue and nibbled her lips caused her to moan. He was a damn good kisser, almost as good as Derrick.

She shivered as Derrick rubbed his cock against her other thigh. He captured her face in his large hands and tore her from Josh's kiss to brand her with his own. Derrick was all heat and man. He still tasted of the wine they'd had with dinner, and his unique masculine flavor.

He kissed her so hard her head spun with the wildness of it. She kissed him back, wanting him, needing him, wishing she could touch him.

Both men had their hands all over her body, touching her breasts, tugging at her nipples, and palming her ass as she continued to kiss Derrick.

"I caught Lauren and Sara fucking a Domme's slave," Josh murmured just before he bit her earlobe. "If that had been you, and I was your Dom, I would have whipped your ass raw."

Andi's eyes widened, and Derrick smiled against her lips. "If I ever catch you with another man without my permission," he said, "you can bet I'll find one hell of a punishment."

She wasn't sure how she felt about what was happening right at this moment, but when Derrick kissed her with fierce intensity, she didn't care about anything but his mouth on hers, his hands on her skin, his cock pressed against her. The feeling of having two men stroking her, kissing her, and rubbing their cocks against her was an experience she never would have imagined. Yet here she was, and it was making her so wet.

As Derrick kissed her, she was aware of Master Josh dropping to his knees in front of her. He rubbed his nose against the small strip of cloth covering her mound and she shivered as he audibly inhaled. "Your slave smells sweet, Derrick." His voice was a low rumble. "I wonder how she tastes."

Derrick pulled away from Andi, his blue eyes fixed on hers. For a moment she thought she saw indecision and jealousy, but then his face became a mask of dominance again.

"Taste her," he told Josh while his gaze held Andi's, and her whole body went weak. Derrick was going to *share* her.

Again.

Just how far they would go, she didn't know.

Why should I care, as long as it feels good?

Derrick captured her mouth again with his, at the same time Josh caught her G-string with his teeth and tugged it down. She felt the scrape of his teeth against the soft skin of her mound, and she groaned into Derrick's mouth.

Master Josh tugged the G-string around her ankles and pulled it free of her heels. He used his hands to part her folds and, at the first swipe of his tongue, she tipped her head back and cried out.

"I—I'm going to come, Master," she whispered.

"*No.*" Derrick took her face in his hands and forced her to look at him. "You will *not* come without permission."

She heard him, but her body didn't want to listen. Her thighs trembled on either side of Master Josh's head and her core ached.

Derrick released her. He moved away and her body screamed for his warmth, his touch—even as Josh licked, sucked, and nibbled at her clit, much like he had her mouth when he'd kissed her.

Her eyes were nearly crossing as she fought against an oncoming climax. Through her blurry vision she saw Sara and Lauren watching, pulling against their own bonds. Strapped to the St. Andrew's cross, Lauren's folds glistened in the torchlight. In her cage, Sara's nipples looked rigid and she was biting her lower lip.

Andi twisted against her bonds, her skin slick with sweat, her mind woozy from hanging from the handcuffs and from what the men had been doing to her. "Master, please," she begged, turning her gaze to where Derrick now stood.

Her body suddenly went cold when she saw the whip in his hand.

Chapter 12

Derrick must have seen the fear in her eyes because his expression softened. He held the handle in one hand and slid the long leather strap through the fingers of his other hand.

"Do you trust me, baby?" His voice was low, but still dominant.

Master Josh lapped her slit one last time, then eased to his feet as Derrick moved behind her.

Andi didn't know whether to feel relieved or disappointed that Josh was no longer licking her.

A wicked grin curved the corner of Josh's mouth and he swooped down to kiss her again. If these men didn't stop kissing her with such intensity, such passion, Andi was going to pass out. Josh's mouth was hot and he tasted of her juices.

But the heat and tenseness radiating from behind her were palpable. Without looking she sensed that Derrick wasn't as cool about sharing her as he had appeared to be.

With a satisfied glint in his eye, Josh stepped back and folded his arms across his broad chest, never taking his gaze from Andi. His cock was large and erect, and she had no doubt he wanted her.

But would Derrick let him have her? Did she want him to?

She didn't have time to think anymore as warm breath stirred the hair at the nape of her neck, and the long leather strip of the whip caressed her flesh.

"I think you enjoyed Master Josh's attentions too much, baby," he said, so low she was sure that only she could hear. "Just remember that you belong to me and me alone."

She couldn't get a word out at first and had to clear her throat. "Yes, Master," she finally said. "Only you."

"Good." His voice held a note of satisfaction and she breathed a sigh of relief that she'd said the right thing. Maybe he would forget the punishment he'd promised her?

He snaked the whip around her body, gently caressing her with it as he moved from behind her then blocked her view of Josh.

She shivered as he continued the slow and sensual movement of the whip over her body. He was all male . . . all intoxicating, hard, hot male. She had to have him so badly she didn't care who watched, and she had to have him now.

"What do you want, baby?" he murmured, anticipating her thoughts, then flicked the whip. It curled around her body like a leather lasso, suddenly capturing her.

She startled, even though there was no pain. With no hesitation, she said, "I want you, Master."

He snapped the whip again, and it curled tighter around her body. "Exactly what do you want of me?"

Andi groaned with need. The sting she felt from the whip this time did nothing but increase her desire. "I want you to fuck me . . . Master."

He gave a low growl of satisfaction and moved away. "I will . . . once you've been punished."

Andi whimpered. She was afraid, she was excited, she was apprehensive, and she was so crazy with lust she could barely hold back a scream.

Derrick stepped back and snapped his wrist. This time the whip stung every place it touched as it wrapped around her belly, her thighs, her calves, and her ankles. She couldn't hold back her cry of surprise at the pain. She blinked back tears but the sting of the whip made her pussy ache more.

"You'll learn to obey me in every way." Derrick snapped his wrist again, and again the whip snaked around her body. "Isn't that right, baby?"

She nodded, fighting back more tears, determined not to cry. He wasn't really hurting her. Even though she was feeling pain, she needed him more than ever.

Derrick smiled in satisfaction at the pink stripes wrapped around Andi's body like a candy cane. He was an expert with the whip and he would never injure her. He could bring her incredible pleasure, bring her to orgasm with it if he chose to.

God, she looked beautiful. She dangled from the handcuffs, the strong lines of her firm body taut as she stretched down to the floor. She was all curves and softness and pure woman. Her dark hair fell about her shoulders and her brown eyes glistened with moisture. Her lips were full and slightly parted, and his cock jerked against his belly when she bit her lower lip.

Josh had moved to the side to watch while Derrick lashed the whip out again and again. The man's jaw was tight, his arms folded so hard against his chest that his elbows were white.

"Master," Andi's voice came out in a choked whisper, "I'm afraid I can't hold back any longer."

"You will." Derrick kept his voice controlled even though he wanted to wrap his arms around her and carry her to his bed. He didn't want to do what they'd planned for her, but he intended to make Andi realize that he was in control and that she would be his. And for this one night she would be pleasured beyond her wildest dreams.

He flung the whip aside and approached Andi. Torchlight flickered across her bare skin.

"Get the glass cock, Josh," Derrick said to his friend, but kept his gaze on Andi.

Her eyes widened, then grew larger when Josh brought a clear crystal cock out of a freezer. The freezer was cleverly hidden in a cabinet that blended in with the room's realistic dungeon look.

Andi shivered and her gaze followed the thing Derrick called a glass cock as Josh handed it to him. Like a perfectly formed penis, it had a thick head and a shaft long enough to make her swallow, wondering if it would fit, and just how deep Derrick intended to thrust it.

He reached her and brushed his lips over hers at the same time he slid the frozen phallus over one nipple and then the other. She groaned into his mouth and shivered. Her body still stung pleasantly from the whipping, and she was so strung out she was about to lose her mind. She felt almost high, like she could float among the clouds, yet grounded at the same time.

Derrick slipped the glass cock along the center of her belly, slowly traveling to her belly button, over her tight abdomen, and down to her moist curls. Shivers skittered throughout her body and she shuddered from his touch and the coldness of the glass.

"Do you want me to fuck you with this?" Derrick asked.

All that came through Andi's lips was a low moan. He raised

an eyebrow and she forced herself to speak. "If it pleases you, Master." She'd rather have his hot cock inside her, but right now she'd take anything to assuage the ache in her pussy.

He gave her a look of approval, slipped the ice-cold glass down through her slit and then shoved it into her channel.

Andi screamed. She pushed her chest out and tipped her head back, the sensation so intense that she couldn't control her reaction.

"That's it, baby," he murmured. "But don't come until I tell you. Remember that."

She whimpered again, and he thrust the glass cock a few times more, in and out of her pussy. Then he withdrew it and brought the still-cold glass to her lips.

"Lick it."

Andi kept her eyes focused on Derrick. Her lips trembled as he slipped the chilled head of the glass cock into her warm mouth. She tasted her essence again, but what turned her on even more was how hotly Derrick's eyes were burning as he thrust the smooth glass in and out of her mouth.

He pulled it away and handed it to Master Josh.

Andi blinked. She'd forgotten about him, about everything but Derrick. Suddenly she was aware of the ache in her arms from having them bound above her head, the fur-lined cuffs around her wrists, Lauren and Sara watching—everything.

She saw Josh take a tube of clear gel and spread it over the glass cock. After he set the tube aside, he moved behind her.

Andi swallowed. Really hard.

Derrick palmed her breasts. "Relax."

She felt the cool head of the thick glass penis against the tight rosette of her ass.

"Don't clench, slave," Josh said in a deep rumble, his warm breath upon her skin causing her to shiver. "It'll go easier for you."

The glass felt slick and filled her, widening her as he pushed it up and into her ass. It was warmer now, her body having heated it, but it was no less stimulating as Josh pumped it in and out of her tight hole. The entire time he fucked her ass with the device, Derrick fondled her, his warm touch driving her to new levels of pleasure.

She sagged against her bonds when Josh finally pulled the glass cock completely out. He set it aside on a wooden table and returned to her.

Both men pressed up against her, Josh behind and Derrick in front of her. Andi went still. This was what they'd been leading up to all along. She'd known it.

She wanted it.

They reached up and unfastened her handcuffs. When she was freed, she went limp, her limbs refusing to hold her up. Derrick murmured soft words she couldn't comprehend in her muddled state of mind. She was crazy with lust, crazy with need, and if she didn't get relief soon she was sure she was going to die.

Derrick held her to him, smashing her breasts against his warm chest as he massaged her arms, which tingled from the rush of blood flowing back through them. Josh rubbed her muscles from behind and she was hyperaware of the two of them touching her. And then they began kissing her.

Derrick held her tight, his mouth hot on hers, his tongue delving into her. But then he withdrew and forced her head to the side where Josh waited. The Dom captured her mouth with his, his kiss harder and fiercer than Derrick's had been.

"Wrap your legs around me," Derrick commanded Andi as Josh broke the kiss.

She braced her hands on Derrick's shoulders, but she was still so weak from all that they had done to her that he had to help her wrap her thighs around his hips.

He moved his mouth to her ear, his breath hot against her face. "I'm going to fuck you, baby. Hard. Real hard."

The fire in Andi's belly grew to an inferno and she moaned. "Yes, Master."

He gripped her ass cheeks with both hands and spread them wide. "Master Josh is going to slide into your tight ass and we're going to fuck you at the same time. It'll feel so good. You're going to love it, baby."

Andi swallowed, but there was no hesitation as she replied, "Yes, Master."

Josh pressed against her backside and rubbed his slick cock up and down her crack. She could feel the condom he'd slipped over his erection. She couldn't hold back another moan as he placed the head at the tight rosette of her ass.

"I've wanted to fuck you since the moment I flogged this sweet ass of yours," Master Josh said in a low rumble that sent impossible thrills through her belly.

At the same time, Derrick palmed her breasts and pinched her nipples so hard she had to bite her lip to keep from crying out at the sweet pain. She clenched her thighs tighter around his hips.

All that male hardness surrounding her was so unbelievably erotic that she was flying high with sensations that were almost too much to bear.

And when Derrick placed the head of his cock at the opening of her channel, she thought she would explode into a million sparkling pieces.

"Fuck me, Master . . . please," she said, not caring that she was begging him.

He gave her a slow, sexy smile that she knew was only for her. "I'll share you this one time, but never again. I want you to feel like you've never felt before."

Andi clenched his shoulders tighter as he spread her ass cheeks even wider.

Josh pressed the head of his cock harder against her hole and grasped her waist with one hand.

And then, in perfect synchronization, both men thrust into her. Andi screamed.

They held still for a moment as she felt herself expanded, filled beyond belief. Two cocks were inside her. Two gorgeous men were about to fuck her senseless.

"That's it," Derrick said as he began thrusting in and out of her pussy.

Josh thrust in tandem. "God, you're tight," he said.

Andi could barely hear, blood was pounding in her ears so hard. Wave after wave of sensation rode through her, threatened to overcome her, to bring her to climax. Somehow she was aware that she couldn't cross that line, that she had to hold back. But her body didn't want to listen.

She fought to hold onto herself, but it was no use. She dissolved, becoming a part of both men as they thrust harder and harder. Their hands gripped her body, their cocks owned her pussy and her ass. Their sweat-slicked flesh slid together and her juices flooded, coating her thighs and Derrick's cock. The smell of sweat, testosterone, and sex filled her senses. The men spoke words so arousing that her mind could barely bend itself around them.

It was all too much to bear. "I can't—" Her voice broke and tears blurred her eyes. "God, I can't hold back. Please let me come, Master."

Derrick thrust harder. "Hold on . . . hold on, baby."

And just when she thought she was going to explode, Derrick shouted, "Come now, Andi. Now!"

Then she did explode. Her body shattered like fine crystal smashed in an earthquake of massive proportions. Pieces of her seemed to fly throughout the room, her senses on complete overload. Her body quaked and quaked and quaked, and she thought her orgasm would never, ever end. She didn't want it to end. It was the most amazing orgasm—the most intense—that she had ever experienced.

Vaguely, she was aware of Derrick's and Josh's shouts and groans as they came. She felt the throb of their cocks within her that only made her own orgasm pulse more.

Both men held her tight, their breathing heavy and matching the rhythm of her own.

At last Josh released her and slid out of her ass. Derrick eased his cock from her channel, then brought her up so that she was cradled in his arms.

Andi snuggled against his chest, unable to think, her breathing still ragged. Derrick brushed his lips over hers and she melted even further against him, totally sated, completely exhausted. And then her eyelids drifted shut and she passed into a deep and complete sleep.

Chapter 13

Sunday morning, Derrick held Andi close in the bed in their master suite. Her body was spooned against his, and his erect cock pressed against her backside. Sunlight streamed onto her perfect features, illuminating her face so that she looked like an angel.

Still she slept, her breathing deep and even, an occasional soft sigh slipping through her lips.

Last night, after he'd taken her back to their suite, he'd allowed her to rest—she'd been so exhausted, it was as if she'd slipped into oblivion. If she hadn't been so tired, he would have made love to her again and again, branding her completely as his own.

She belonged to him.

He snuggled closer to her, enjoying the feel of her in his arms. His chin rested on her mussed hair, his arm cradling her slim waist.

The emotions that ranged through him surprised him with their intensity. He had shared women with Josh before, but this time had been harder. Andi wasn't just any woman. Sharing her had been Derrick's way of showing her that she was his to control.

But he realized the truth. *She* controlled *him*. She made him wild with need and lust . . . and maybe even love.

He pressed his lips to her hair, breathing in her jasmine perfume and her scent of pure woman.

Andi stirred and sighed again. Derrick propped himself on one elbow and traced his finger down her shoulder to her elbow and back, and she shivered in her sleep. Her nipples puckered against the silk sheet draped over her breasts and over the curve of her hip. Only her bare feet peeked out from beneath the cream silk.

He leaned down and blew into her ear. A soft smile tipped the corner of her lips and then she opened her eyes, slowly blinking away the morning light.

"Derrick?" she murmured as she turned in his arms to face him. She frowned as if trying to remember something, and then said, "Oh. I mean, Master."

He smiled and ran the pad of his finger down to the tip of her nose. "Let's just be Derrick and Andi today, okay?"

She returned his smile, only hers was so radiant it seemed to light up the already sunny room.

"All right." Her movement was bold as she reached up and pushed a lock of his hair from his face. "Does that mean I can do whatever I want to you?"

Just the thought of her having her way with him made him groan. "Baby, I'm yours."

She gave an impish grin and slid her hand over his stubbled cheek, down his chest, and under the sheet. When she reached his naked cock, she wrapped her small fingers around his erection and he groaned again.

Before he lost all rational thought, he had to get something off his mind, something he'd wanted to tell her all weekend. He caught her hand and brought it to his chest, pressing it over his heart.

"We need to talk," he said.

Andi blinked. His face was so serious that for a moment she was afraid he was going to tell her their weekend was over already, and it was time to part ways. Why that bothered her so much, she wasn't sure, but she did know she wasn't ready for the weekend to end.

But come Monday . . .

Derrick grasped her hand tighter in his, his penetrating blue gaze focused on her. "I'm falling in love with you."

Andi's eyes widened. Her heart raced and heat flushed straight to her head, making her dizzy with it. "You—"

"I'm serious." He released her hand to cup the side of her face. He rubbed his thumb from her lips, across her cheek and back. "I can't get enough of you, Andi. I don't think I ever will. I can't imagine not waking up with you every day of my life."

She closed her eyes and took a deep breath. This was not happening. She did not want this.

But her heart ached at his words, and a desire rose up even fiercer than sexual need. The desire to be with Derrick—maybe even to love him one day.

"Talk to me, baby." His voice was low, almost hesitant.

Andi opened her eyes to meet his straightforward gaze. She knew that with Derrick there would never be falseness or lies. He was a good and honest man.

"This is nuts," she said. "You can't love me."

"Why not?" A grin curved the corner of his mouth. "I've admired you from the moment I met you. And I've always wanted you."

Andi looked up at him from beneath her lashes. "I've wanted you, too. But love . . ."

He moved his hand from her face to her long hair and wrapped it around his fingers. "All I ask is that you give us a chance. Give what we have a chance to grow and we'll go from there."

She took a deep breath and slowly released it. *Wow*. He wasn't asking for commitment. He was just asking for her to give them time to build a relationship—if that's what she really wanted.

Somehow with Derrick the thought of a serious relationship didn't cause her to want to run the other way. Somehow it felt right. It felt good.

Warmth spread through her and she felt it radiating from her soul. She couldn't help but smile. "Maybe I'm falling in love with you, too."

Derrick's smile was so devastatingly sexy that it nearly caused her to melt into a pool of lust and need, and maybe even something deeper, that love thing they were talking about.

"But no pressure, okay?"

"No pressure," he said, but he had a wicked gleam in his eyes. "Just know that I don't intend to let you go."

Andi shivered at the note of possession in his voice. Before she had a chance to respond, he caught her mouth in a hard, fierce kiss. She couldn't believe how much she wanted him, how much she wanted to love him.

Derrick eased between her thighs. She arched her hips up to meet him, enjoying the press of his cock against her belly, the feel of his weight, his hot flesh, his warm breath feathering across her lips.

Derrick kissed his woman, knowing that he could never let her go. He would give her the time she needed to realize she was his, and that she loved him.

He eased down Andi's body, brushing his lips along the line of her jaw and down the curve of her neck. She made sweet little moans as he kissed and licked his way to the valley between her breasts, tasting the salt of her skin and breathing in the scent of her. She was soft and warm, sweet and pliant.

"Suck my nipples," she said in her low, breathless voice.

He chuckled against her breast and licked a path to her nipple. He sucked, hard, and she cried out and squirmed beneath him. "Yeah, like that," she said, and he moved his mouth so that he could bite her other tight bud.

She clenched her hands in his hair, pulling at it so that he felt it all the way down to the roots, so hard it was almost painful. He liked it, liked the way she was losing control beneath him, thrashing and crying out.

He wanted to drive into her now, but he held back, teasing her by slowly moving down the line of her belly and to her mound.

"You are so damn sexy, baby." He blew his breath against her belly button, and she squirmed. He smelled her musk, the scent of their sex.

He nuzzled her soft curls and groaned. His cock was beyond hard, but he had to taste her, had to give her pleasure.

It was a need that gripped him and wouldn't let go. It wasn't about him. This was about *her* pleasure, making Andi feel how much he cared for her.

He licked her clit and she clenched her hands impossibly tighter in his hair and he licked her harder.

Andi felt even hotter than she had the other times they'd fucked. But the fact that he'd told her he was falling in love with her made every one of her senses seem more alive than ever before.

Maybe this was what making love was like.

His stubble scraped the insides of her thighs and the lips of her folds as he laved her over and over. He plunged his fingers into her slick core as he licked her clit, and she pumped her hips against his face.

"I'm so close to coming, Derrick," she said, barely able to breathe.

"Come for me, baby," he murmured against her pussy, then nipped her clit.

Andi cried out. She arched up off the bed with the force of her climax. It rushed from her belly through every part of her body.

She was almost sobbing from the impact of the orgasm when Derrick rose up, braced his hands to either side of her head, and plunged his cock inside her.

Andi shouted again, more aftershocks causing her core to clench around his cock. He held himself still for a moment just staring down at her. His dark hair fell across his forehead. The angular curve of his jaw was tense and his blue eyes were dark with desire.

He rose up, hooked his arms under her knees, and put her ankles to either side of his neck. He planted his hands beside her head and began to rock, thrusting his hips up hard but slowly. So deep, he felt so deep, and he touched a spot far down inside her that had never been reached before. Every thrust of his cock caused her to tremble and squirm and pulse around him.

Derrick looked down between their bodies, and her gaze followed to see his cock sliding in and out of her. The sight was so erotic that she climaxed again, her hips bucking and trembling.

"That's it, baby." He rocked harder, drawing out her climax.

And when she came yet another time, he finally shouted with an orgasm that was so powerful his entire body shook against hers.

He braced himself above her for a moment, his head thrown back, looking like a god in the throes of passion.

Slowly, he eased her legs down and rolled to his side, bringing her with him and his cock slipped from her core.

They cuddled together and she sank into his embrace, enjoying the strength of him against her. Their bodies were slick with sweat and the scent of sex surrounded them. Andi had never felt more content or more cared for in her life.

Derrick smiled and kissed her softly. "You're mine, baby. You know that, don't you?"

She couldn't help a smile of happiness. "I'm all yours."

Forbidden
Surrender

❧

Chapter 1

Teri tossed her briefcase on the hotel bed and barely resisted throwing herself on it as well. God, she was tired and up-tight. "Your problem, Teri Carter," she said with a sigh, "is that you *really* need to get laid."

Did she *ever*. It had been ages since she'd had a man, but her advancement in her career as a corporate lawyer had really put the skids on her sex life. She didn't have time to date, was never in one place long enough to really meet anyone who met her strict criteria—a good bank account so that he wouldn't live off of *her*; decent looks; great sex. A real man's man. Someone who could hold his own, especially with her. So far she hadn't dated any man who really could.

Ugh. Wimps.

Teri rubbed her temples with her fingertips. Her head and back ached, and her shoulders were tense from yet another long flight. She traveled so much it was a wonder she even remembered what city she was in.

She kicked off her flats and padded over the plush carpet to the expansive window of the executive suite. She drew open the curtain to reveal an incredible view of the Golden Gate Bridge and Alcatraz from her San Francisco hotel. She could just imagine being out on the wharf now, breathing in the salty, briny smell of the water, feeling the moist air upon her skin, hearing the screech of gulls and the bark of sea lions.

A tired smile touched her lips. Too bad she was only here for business, not for pleasure. Her intense schedule didn't give her any room for relaxation.

Teri let the curtain drop and turned away from the view. She unbuttoned her silk blouse and the material slid down in a cool and sensual whisper against her skin. She was so tired she didn't bother to pick it up. Instead, she left a trail of clothing from the bedroom into the bathroom as she stripped from her bra, her slacks, and her panties.

When she was naked, she paused at the mirror and studied her reflection. Her features were tight and drawn, her makeup barely concealing the shadows under her eyes.

She reached up and took the clip from her hair, which tumbled to her shoulders in a long, brunette mass. After tossing her clip to the marble countertop she ran her fingers through her hair and massaged her scalp. The movement caused her breasts to rise and her gaze dropped to nipples that were the color of pink carnations.

Slowly, she moved her hands from her hair and lowered them to her breasts. Her breathing quickened as she pinched her nipples between her thumbs and forefingers. The erotic feeling made her nubs tighten and she grew damp between her thighs.

Teri watched herself in the mirror, her eyes growing heavy-lidded as a fantasy weaved its way through her mind. She imagined a stranger pressed up against her ass, his erection firm against her backside. His hands pinched and pulled at her nipples. His touch made her wet, craving his cock.

She slid one hand slowly from her breast, down her flat belly to the trimmed curls between her thighs. She cupped herself as the stranger would, before slipping a finger into her moist folds.

While she rubbed her clit, she never took her gaze off her reflection. She saw the flush steal over her skin as she drew herself closer to climax, watching the way her hand moved against her mound and how her other hand continued to roll and pinch her nipple.

She imagined the stranger's warm mouth between her legs now, the feel of his tongue against her folds, his head between her thighs. The image was so powerful that her finger circled her clit faster and faster.

Teri came with a jerk of her hips against her hand and a rush of heat through her body. She continued fingering her clit as waves of pleasure washed over her. She had to move her other hand from her breast to the countertop to brace herself. Still she watched while her body trembled as her orgasm continued on, and she bit her lower lip as she met her green eyes in the mirror.

When the last pulse of her climax eased away she slipped her fingers from her folds, brought them to her nose, and inhaled. Sex. The smell of sex was so good. Even better when mixed with the musky scent of a man.

Teri placed both hands on the countertop and this time closed her eyes. What would it *really* be like to lose all inhibitions and have sex with a stranger? She wouldn't even have to know his name. He'd just have to fuck her good and hard, and leave her satisfied.

She sighed, opened her eyes, and pushed away from the mirror. Did she dare make her fantasy a reality?

After taking a shower, putting on fresh makeup, fixing her hair, and taking care of a few necessities, Teri headed to the hotel's bar instead of dialing up room service as usual. She could use a good drink more than a good meal. Rather than dressing casually, though, she had slipped into a little black backless cocktail dress with a halter top and a skirt that reached midthigh. She always traveled with two evening dresses, in case she had dinner appointments with clients or had business functions to attend. One cocktail dress in her luggage was fairly modest, but this one was a little more daring.

In a tiny black purse, Teri had her room key card, credit card, lipstick, cash, and a small package of condoms she'd purchased in the hotel gift shop. A girl had to be prepared.

Her skin heated at the thought of her plan for the night. She couldn't believe she was going through with this. She intended to have a drink or two in the hotel lounge, then find out where one of the local hot spots was. She had every intention of making her fantasy come true.

Sex. With a stranger. Tonight.

When she reached the lounge, her gaze scanned the crowd. Businessmen in suits and ties, other men in casual slacks and polo shirts, none of them remotely interesting. Teri didn't even bother looking at the women in the room.

She found herself a small table in a dim corner of the lounge and signaled for the waitress. As she settled back in one of the cushioned chairs, she tried to relax. Her skin tingled all over from the warm shower she'd taken and she could smell the light scent of her plumeria perfume. She barely had anything on beneath her tiny black dress—just a skimpy lace bra and a thong—and with every movement she made, the silky material of her dress slid across her skin and made her thong damper.

She'd finished two Cosmopolitans to shore up her courage before heading to a nightclub . . . when she saw *him*.

A man straight out of her fantasies.

He walked into the bar with confidence—perhaps even arrogance—in his expression and in his stride. Immediately she had no doubt he was a man who knew what he wanted . . . and got it.

The man had blond hair that curled slightly at the nape of his neck, and he was dressed all in black from his T-shirt to his jeans. God, she loved men in black, and she loved the way his jeans molded his ass. It struck her as extremely sexy that he wasn't wearing slacks like the rest of the men in the bar. He looked rougher. Edgier.

He was handsome in a powerful sort of way that made her mouth dry. Those firm lips. That sexy mouth. She could just imagine . . . jeez. What *couldn't* she imagine with this man?

Her fantasy reached the bar and casually leaned against it. After he got the bartender's attention and placed his order, he turned slightly and his gaze raked the room. Her heart pounded a little harder as she focused on him, waiting for him to look at her. She didn't intend to play coy. She wanted this man.

The moment their eyes met, she felt a jolt from her nipples to her sex. She couldn't have looked away from him even if she wanted to.

Josh Williams studied the brunette. She had large, beautiful green eyes and full lips, and her black dress revealed just enough to entice.

Her fingers slowly slid up and down the stem of her martini glass as she focused on him, and he could easily imagine that small hand stroking his cock.

As a Dom, Josh had more than enough experience in self-control, but at that moment his cock chose to ignore him and to harden painfully against his tight jeans.

This woman was going to have to pay for arousing him with a mere look, a mere movement. In that moment's perusal he had no doubt she wanted him, and she would desire all that he could teach her, do to her, and more.

He had just ended his Dom/sub relationship with the twins, Lauren and Sara. He needed something more than a playful relationship. Something that he couldn't quite define. He'd decided to remove his collars from both women. They'd begged, pleaded that he remain their Dom, but his gut told him it was time to move on.

With practiced ease, Josh kept all emotion from his expression as he studied the green-eyed brunette. The bartender set a beer bottle on the counter beside Josh, and he turned away from the woman just long enough to pay. He held the cool bottle in his hand and without hesitation strode through the maze of tables filled with bar patrons, heading straight for the woman.

Her eyes never left his, but her tongue darted out to lick her lower lip in a nervous movement. Yet her chin was raised and she had an almost haughty look on her face. He would break her of that—and she would love just exactly how he was going to do it. His experienced gaze saw her quickened breathing, the flush in her cheeks, the taut nipples against the silk of her dress. She hadn't even met him, and she was primed and ready.

When he reached her table, he didn't bother to ask if the chair next to her was free. He slid into it, close enough so that his jean-clad thigh brushed the wispy softness of her dress. He set the beer on the table and studied her. She was gorgeous, and he could just imagine how all that soft, pale skin would look with his brand upon it. He caught her womanly scent followed by her perfume that reminded him of plumeria flowers in Hawaii. He couldn't wait to taste her.

A blush tinged her cheeks, and he knew in that moment that this was something she had never done before. "I'm Teri," she said in a soft voice that caused his balls to tighten.

Yes, she was going to pay for the reaction his body was having to her, and she was going to enjoy every minute of it.

Teri held her breath as she waited for the man to respond. This was crazy. What was she doing?

"Josh," he finally said. His voice was deep and sexy enough to make her toes curl. "Tell me about yourself, Teri."

A small shiver raced down her spine at the sound of her name coming from him and the intense look in his gray eyes. His words weren't casual. No, they were commanding. A demand, not a request.

If she were at work, she'd use her tongue like a whip and bring the man to his knees with her frosty attitude. But she wasn't working right now. . . .

Instead of putting her off with his domineering attitude, Teri wanted to squirm in her chair from the ache his request caused between her thighs. His musky male scent and the clean smell of aftershave made her want to wrap herself around him.

"Tell me, Teri," he commanded again, this time with an almost disapproving look in his eyes.

She didn't know what compelled her most, but perhaps it was

the incredible desire burning inside her from just being near this stranger. "I'm a corporate lawyer," she said with a tilt of her head, challenging him. "I don't take orders well."

A slow smile curved one corner of his mouth. He reached up and gently stroked her bare upper arm. Goose bumps prickled her skin. "I can teach you how to take orders and love every minute of it."

She tilted her head to one side and did her best to sound casual. "How?"

"First tell me about you." He leaned closer to her, one forearm braced on the table. "What makes you tick?"

She raised her chin a little higher. "I'm a Harvard graduate, VP in charge of corporate negotiations—"

"*You*, Teri," he said more firmly, his gray eyes snapping with something electric. The way he kept repeating her name unnerved her. Like he was interrogating her, expecting her to cave and spill her guts. The bug-under-the-microscope trick. She almost laughed. She knew that ploy well. Yet she didn't find it offensive. In fact, she found it stimulating.

All right, if this was how the game was going to be played. "I live in Los Angeles by myself. I don't even have a cat because I travel so much."

He slid his fingers along her forearm. "That's not who you really are."

"What do you want? My panty size?" Teri said, hearing the defiance in her voice.

"Later." Josh studied her more intently. "Now tell me about *you*." Later?

"My favorite color is yellow," she tossed out. "I like to jog, to go sailing, and to spend time with my sister's kids when I can. Which isn't often since they live in Minneapolis."

At this he gave her a more approving look and his gray eyes focused on her mouth. "What is your deepest, darkest desire? What is it you want more than anything right now? Right this minute."

She went stock still. Heat crept up her neck. She couldn't speak.

He leaned close enough that she could have kissed him. When he spoke next she felt the warmth of his breath against her lips and caught the pleasant, yeasty scent of beer. "What do you want right now, Teri?" he repeated.

"I—" Her throat was so dry she could hardly get anything out. When she did, she couldn't believe the words came out of her mouth, but it was as if he was magically drawing them from her. "I want to be fucked by a stranger." A wash of heat flushed over her. She was a tough lawyer, but this—this was different.

Josh gave a nod of approval at her honesty, but his expression was still unreadable. "Just any stranger?"

Her whole body was on fire with embarrassment, arousal, and yet confidence, too. "I want to be fucked by you."

Chapter 2

Teri almost slapped her hand over her mouth. She'd just told a stranger she wanted him to fuck her.

"Good girl." Josh brushed his lips so softly over hers that she gasped. "You'll be rewarded for your honesty."

Before she had a chance to process that comment, he leaned back. "Tell me how you like to be fucked."

She blinked. Tried to think more clearly. Okay, time to change things up a bit. "It's only fair you tell me about yourself, first."

He gave a slow nod. "Fair is fair."

"What are you doing here in San Francisco?" She felt a little more on familiar ground doing the interrogating. "What do you do for a living?"

"I'm in the city for a conference," he said. "I own a stock brokerage."

Ten points for Josh. "Where do you live?" she asked.

He took a swig of his beer. "Born and raised in Los Angeles."

She felt a strange sort of pleasure that they shared the same city. "Angels or Dodgers?"

Josh grinned. "Dodgers, through and through."

"Humph." She tapped her manicured nails on the table. "You just lost points on that one."

He chuckled and then answered her other questions. He had two sisters, a brother, and a puppy named Stix.

"What about relationships?" she asked. "Any girlfriends in the closet?"

He didn't seem to mind her straightforwardness as he gave just as direct of an answer. "I just ended a yearlong relationship with Lauren and Sara."

Her eyes widened. "*Two* women?"

He shrugged one shoulder. "They're twins."

"Every man's fantasy," Teri murmured.

"But tonight you're my fantasy, Teri," he said. Then he gave her what was most definitely a command. "Remove your underwear."

She jerked and her hand bumped into her empty martini glass, knocking it over. In a fast movement, Josh caught the glass and righted it. "Are you out of your mind?" she said in a harsh whisper.

He raised a brow, challenging her.

Teri's mind raced as her body grew hotter. Take off her underwear—in public—for a stranger?

First off she had to rethink that *stranger* part.

Well, that had been one of her goals and she'd scored—and with a pretty damned hot stranger.

But still.

"I can't do that," she said as low as possible. "What if someone sees?"

He narrowed his eyes and she widened hers. "Now, Teri."

She swallowed. His gaze unnerved her, at the same time the

look in his eyes excited her, intoxicated her. This man was all about control and domination—something she'd fantasized about how many times? Letting a man take control. . . .

Teri took a deep breath.

She inched her hand up one side of her skirt to her hip, until her fingers reached the edge of her thong. Adrenaline rushed through her body at the thought of getting caught. She glanced around the bar to see if anyone could see what she was doing.

"Look at me, Teri, and don't look away again."

Her gaze snapped back to him and she met his gray eyes. Butterflies began battling the insides of her belly like crazy, and her body hummed. She forced herself to watch him as she inched her underwear from her hips. She prayed the tablecloth was long enough that no one could see her move her thong down her thighs to her knees, where it promptly fell to her ankles. With her cheeks burning like crazy, she caught the edge of her thong with the toe of her high heel, and brought it up high enough that she could grasp it with her hand. It was totally damp.

When she had it in her lap, he held out his open palm. "Give it to me."

Fine. She raised it and flung it at him like a slingshot.

Amusement flashed across his features as he snatched it out of the air. He raised the thong to his nose, and she watched his chest rise as he inhaled. "You're hot for me, aren't you," he said— a statement, not a question.

She shifted in her seat, aware of how much more naked she was beneath her dress. She waited two heartbeats before she said, "Yes."

He took her underwear and stuffed it into his back pocket. "Yes, what?"

She wrinkled her brows, puzzled. "What do you mean?"

He looked at her and said in a calm, matter-of-fact way, "Yes, Master."

This time Teri almost upset the whole table, the way her body jerked in surprise. "Yes, *Master?*"

"That's right, Teri." He leaned in close once again, and moved his lips to her ear. His warm breath caressed her as he said, "Tonight I'm your Master."

Master? Wasn't that something that a submissive called a Dominant in a BDSM relationship? "Are you out of your freaking mind?" she asked in disbelief.

He reached up and brushed the heavy fall of her dark hair over her shoulder, his fingers grazing her bare skin and causing tingles to radiate through her. "Tonight I'll be your Master. Turn over control to me and I'll give you a night you'll never forget."

"Are you a Dom?" she asked, keeping her voice steady. "Are you into BDSM?"

"That's right." He laid his hand over her thigh and stroked her bare skin with his thumb. "And I intend to fuck you in ways you've never been fucked before."

She took a deep breath. "I'm not so sure about this."

"I think you are." His hand slowly moved up her leg, pushing the silky material of her dress up to her hip.

She couldn't move for the life of her as his fingers met the crevice between her thigh and her pussy. His eyes held hers the entire time he touched her. When his fingers slipped into her wet folds she nearly lost it.

Her entire body was trembling as he gave a satisfied smile. "You want me to fuck you so bad that you'd take me right here, right now, wouldn't you." Another statement.

"I, uh—" Where'd her brain just go?

"*Yes, Master,*" he said calmly as he began to stroke her clit.

She could barely think as his fingers dipped in and out of her slick core and then moved back to her clit. She was pretty sure the tablecloth covered them enough so that no one could see what he was doing to her, but she was afraid anyone in the bar could read it in her expression.

"You're going to climax in front of all these people," he said in a firm voice. "Do you understand?"

God, she didn't want him to stop.

It was all she could do not to start moaning aloud. "Yes, Master," she whispered. Master? Did she really just called this stranger Master?

He gave her an approving smile. "Very good."

His gaze never leaving hers, Josh thrust two fingers into her pussy and she almost yelped from the exquisite feel of it. With expert movements, he stroked her wet folds, then began to concentrate on her clit, circling it, moving in slow, drawn-out movements.

She was going to lose her mind. Her eyelids began to drift closed, but his sharp voice brought her gaze snapping back to his. "Look at me," he demanded. "Watch me while I finger fuck you."

The intense look in his icy gray eyes made the feelings build up even more and more within her. She was close, so close.

"Come *now*, Teri," he commanded at the same time he pinched her clit, *hard*.

Her body exploded. She couldn't help the moan that rushed through her lips as her hips bucked against his hand and a light sheen of sweat broke out over her skin. Her body shook as he continued holding onto her clit.

When she couldn't take any more, she said, "Josh. Stop."

He pinched harder and her body jerked again. "Yes?"

"Um—please, Master." She couldn't believe she was saying this. "Please stop, Master."

He gave her a satisfied smile and withdrew his hand from her pussy. She almost collapsed in exhaustion from the incredible orgasm she'd just had. Even the pain of him pinching her clit had made her climax more exquisite.

Josh brought his hand to his nose and inhaled again, and she saw her juices glistening on his fingers. He slipped first one and then another into his mouth.

What a turn-on.

"You taste delicious." He picked up a napkin from the tabletop and wiped his fingers clean. "I want to sample more of you."

Her body was completely buzzing with desire and need. He'd already given her an amazing orgasm. What else could he do for her?

Josh took her hand, catching her by surprise, and brought her up with him to stand. He picked up her little black purse and handed it to her. "We're going to my room," he said in a matter-of-fact tone.

It was as if she was in a dream. Her legs barely felt like they would support her after her orgasm. She couldn't believe that this stranger had such immediate control over her. Within fifteen minutes of meeting her, he'd had her underwear off and had finger fucked her. And now she was letting him take her to his room.

As Josh led her through the crowded hotel lounge, Teri's heart pounded, and countless thoughts raced through her mind. *What was she doing? Where was he taking her? Was she out of her mind? This was a stranger. What if he was dangerous?*

But that dangerous mien about him was what made her more excited. It was controlled danger that made her want to experience all that he had to offer. He was definitely a bad boy, and that turned her on big time. Instinct told her that this man wouldn't harm her . . . but what if her instincts were wrong?

It was too late to back out. She wanted him too badly. She'd wanted to be fucked by a stranger tonight, and that's exactly what she was going to get.

But a Dom? A BDSM Master? What did he have in mind for her?

Rather than frighten her, the thought intrigued her. She knew about BDSM, knew that a submissive relinquished control to the Dominant. Did she want that for tonight? As a corporate lawyer, she was used to being in control. Could she turn that over to this man?

Josh had such a hard-on that he had to bite the inside of his cheek to control the need to take Teri the moment they stepped into his hotel room. Hell, he would have taken her in the elevator if he didn't have other plans for her.

He gripped her hand in his as they walked across the hotel lobby. He looked down at her and gave her a reassuring yet dominant look to let her know exactly what her place was in this night's relationship.

"You'll have a safe word, Teri," he said as they reached the bank of elevators. "If at any time you want me to stop, you say the word and it's over."

She cleared her throat. "Safe word?"

"Master," he reminded her with a low rumble.

"Yes, er, Master."

"Choose a word, Teri."

They reached the elevators and Josh pressed the up button while Teri looked as if she was trying to think of something.

"Negotiations," she finally said.

He nodded and held back a smile as the elevator door dinged. "*Negotiations* it is."

Even though there would be no negotiations tonight.

The elevator was empty, to Josh's satisfaction, and it was glass-walled. He pressed his hand to her lower back, and ushered her into it as he let his palm slide down the silky dress over her ass and guided her so that her back was to him. She gave a startled little gasp and he squeezed her right cheek.

When the door closed behind them he pressed the button for the thirty-first floor. He pushed her up against the wooden bar just below the windows that looked out at the night view of the San Francisco skyline and she gave a little cry of surprise. His body was flush against hers, his erect cock firm against her backside.

As the elevator started to move, Josh shoved her skirt up to her hips, completely baring her ass.

She tugged it back down. "Someone could see!"

"That's your first punishment, Teri." He forced her skirt back up. "You fought me, and you didn't refer to me as Master."

The tough-as-nails lawyer went still, and he wondered if she was about to say her safe word. But instead she gripped the wooden bar as the elevator whooshed upward.

"Pinch your nipples," he commanded as he slipped his fingers into her wet pussy from behind.

In the reflection in the glass he saw her heavy-lidded eyes. "Yes, Master," she said as she brought her hands to her breasts and began tugging at her nipples, pinching and pulling at them.

The elevator came to a stop and dinged, and Josh casually looked over his shoulder to see that they'd arrived at his floor. He let her skirt slide down her ass, but not before he gave one more flick against her clit.

"Oh, jeez," she whispered. As he turned her around to face him, she dropped her hands from her breasts, gave him a cocky look, and said, "I mean, oh, jeez, *Master*."

He almost laughed aloud. Instead he kept his expression stony. A good Dom maintained control at all times. And he was one of the best.

Josh took her by the hand again, and led her onto the carpeted floor and down the hall to his luxury suite, one of the largest in the hotel. He slipped the key card from his pocket and unlocked the door, pushing it open and motioning to Teri to enter.

"Beautiful room," she said in an appreciative voice, "er, Master."

It had a breathtaking view of the Golden Gate Bridge, Alcatraz, and other sights. The windows were floor-to-ceiling and the curtains were wide open. The suite was expansive, with deep, plush carpeting, fine mahogany furniture, and vases of fresh flowers.

When he had her at the center of the room he positioned her so that she was looking at him. He took her small purse from her grip and tossed it onto one of the overstuffed couches.

"Remove your clothing," he commanded.

Teri seriously thought about running for the door. God, would her body ever stop feeling like it was bursting into flames? This time prickles of heat went from her scalp to her toes and back again.

"Teri . . ." he said with a look in his eye that told her she was about to be in serious trouble. He'd said she'd already earned one punishment. No doubt he'd be happy to add another.

Punishments? She was *really* out of her mind to let things go even this far.

"I believe only in safe, sane, and consensual BDSM. If you've changed your mind, say your safe word and everything ends." He rubbed his hands lightly up and down her arms. "Or turn yourself over completely for tonight. I won't accept anything less than absolute submission."

For once Teri hesitated. She was used to making snap decisions, to being in control. From this point on she would relinquish that control to Josh, a Dom she didn't even know.

She'd wanted sex with a stranger, and this man turned her on more than any man ever had in her life. This was her fantasy come true. And if he pushed her too far she'd say her safe word.

When she made up her mind, she made up her mind.

"Yes, Master," she said clearly. "I'm yours for tonight, as long as you promise not to push me too far."

He studied her and slowly nodded. "If I push you beyond your limits, just say your safe word."

When she started to toe off one of her heels, he placed a hand on her arm. "Leave the shoes."

"Yes, Master." She reached behind her for the zipper at the top of her buttocks, and it made a soft hiss as she pulled it down. She maintained eye contact with him as she reached up for the clasp of the dress's halter top. After a heartbeat she let the material drop. It slid down her breasts, her belly, her thighs—a caress against her skin. When it was on the floor, she was bare except for her bra and heels.

He looked at her expectantly. She raised her chin and brought her hands up to unfasten the front clasp of her strapless bra. She let it drop to the floor.

She was entirely naked. In front of a stranger. At this Dom's mercy.

His expression was still unreadable as he slowly walked around her, his gaze taking her in from head to toe. The only sign that he was aroused was the bulge in his jeans, and that gave her a measure of satisfaction. At least she was having some effect on him.

And was he ever having an effect on her. Her nipples were diamond-hard in the cool air of the luxurious suite, and her pussy was so wet her upper thighs were slick from it. She felt completely erotic standing in her three-inch heels and nothing else, with an incredibly gorgeous man studying her body.

He finally came to stand in front of her, and his icy gray eyes focused on her. "Widen your stance to shoulder-width apart, put your hands behind your back and keep your eyes lowered. Don't move until I get back."

Despite her instinct to rebel, she obeyed. "Yes, Master," she mumbled as an afterthought.

Even though her eyes were lowered, she saw him turn away and stride across the plush carpeting to an open door. Through it she could see an enormous bed, and her pussy ached at the thought that this stranger would probably be fucking her on that bed soon.

It seemed to take forever before he returned. Her steel nerves were quickly turning to tinfoil and she was afraid her knees would give out.

And when she saw what he was carrying, they almost did.

Chapter 3

Teri's eyes widened as her head shot up and her jaw dropped. Josh was carrying a black duffel bag in one hand—and a flogger in the other.

Now's the time to run, she shouted in her head.

"You've earned a second punishment," he said as he dropped the duffel bag at her feet. "I told you to keep your eyes lowered."

Oh, shit.

Automatically, as if she'd done this countless times, she looked at the floor and said, "Yes, Master."

He knelt before the duffel bag, in her line of sight, and she studied him while he was intent on searching the bag. He was gorgeous with his blond hair and the way his muscles rippled beneath the taut black T-shirt he wore.

She bit her lip as she watched him draw out a black satin scarf, leather cuffs, a long silver chain with clamps on both ends, a metal-studded black collar, and then what looked like a briefcase.

He opened the briefcase and she gasped. It looked like it was filled with *torture devices*. Glass bulbs that probably attached to those things that looked like fat black pencils.

Oh. My. God.

He started to raise his head and she immediately looked at her feet. She suddenly felt so vulnerable in front of this man. She *was* vulnerable.

When she looked up she could see he was holding only the black collar. "Tonight you are my slave, Teri." He brought the leather to her neck and began fastening it.

Teri almost shouted *"What?"* but bit her tongue to keep from saying anything. Now he was calling her "slave"? When the collar was firm around her neck, she had to resist reaching up to touch it. She'd seen that it had a D ring on it, and the thought went through her mind that he might intend to leash her. How humiliating would that be if he did?

But first things first. She might just run from the room before he had a chance to leash her. "Before I agree to be your slave, will you tell me what that torture kit is?"

"Another fair question." He went to the kit and drew out one of the glass attachments and one of the black fat pencil-looking things. He connected the bulb to the black thing. It had a long cord and he plugged it in as her eyes widened. "It's not a torture kit. It's a 'violet wand,' with several attachments that give you different kinds of pleasure," he said just before it started to pulse with a soft purple glow, like a neon sign.

She licked her lips, feeling shaky to her toes. "What does it do?"

"It's electronic, and adds to the kink in BDSM." He brought it closer to her. "Depending on what kind of sensation you want, it can tingle or it can shock you just enough to feel very good."

Teri started when he trailed the wand down her upper arm.

Then she relaxed into the sensation that was like fizzy cola being poured over her arm, only a little more intense. The idea of it being used on her erotically seemed to make the tingles go straight to her sex. She saw him adjust the wand, then a harsher shock traveled through her body that made her jump.

He gave her a slow, sexual smile. "Just imagine the things I'll do to you with this."

Her imagination was rocketing from the exciting tingling to the greater shock, and she wasn't sure what to think. But then it probably felt better than a flogger.

"Tonight you're mine and I'll use this on you." His look was dominating again, serious. "Do you understand?"

"Yes, Master," she said in a choked voice.

Next he set down the violet wand and selected the satin scarf. Her heartbeat sped up when he brought it to her eyes and began to tie it around her head. She gasped as everything went black.

"This is part of your punishment, slave," he said as he tightened the scarf, just enough so that it was secure and wasn't hurting her. "You've lost the right to see what I'm going to do to you."

"What are you doing to me, Master?" she asked, the words barely coming out in a croak.

"Did I say you could talk, slave?" His fingers grasped her nipple and pinched so hard she yelped.

"No, Master."

"If you talk again without my permission, I'll have to gag you as well."

Her cheeks burned fiery hot, but she didn't open her mouth. A gag was the last thing she wanted.

Blindfolded and unable to see, she found that her other senses

seemed magnified. She could smell his clean scent of man and aftershave, and felt the heat of his body close to hers. When he
moved away she knew it immediately, even though he wasn't
touching her. She imagined him picking up one of the things
he'd laid out on the floor, and then he was standing close to her
again.

"On your knees, slave."

She barely remembered to keep her mouth shut as she followed his instructions. Her high heels wobbled as she tried to
kneel with her hands behind her back. Josh held her elbow and,
with his help, she got to her knees.

"That's a good slave," he murmured as he moved behind her.
The next thing she knew he had taken her wrists and fastened
leather cuffs around each, then hooked them together so that she
couldn't move them.

A raw burst of panic echoed like a firecracker in her chest.
She'd thought she was vulnerable before, but now she was bound
and on her knees, on top of being naked and blindfolded. For
what seemed the millionth time she asked herself what she'd gotten into.

But she'd never been so aroused in her entire life. Her breasts
were hard and aching, her sex so wet that she caught her own
scent.

"You're here to please me." He moved from behind her and
she felt him kneel again in front of her. "Anything I do to you is
for *my* pleasure, not yours."

When I get my hands uncuffed—

Teri started to answer, but remembered his instructions in
time and just nodded.

"As your Master, I know what's best for you. I know what you
need and I'll take care of you."

Teri licked her dry lips and said nothing.

She couldn't help a gasp when something clamped down on her nipple. The pain was incredible, and tears wet her eyes behind the blindfold.

Blinded, she couldn't see what it was, but at the sound of a chain rustling she realized what the silver chain and the two clamps on it were for, just before a clamp bit down on her other nipple.

This time she did cry out in pain, and her eyes watered even more. The pain blended into a strange sense of pleasure. Incredibly, her arousal grew, and she wanted his cock in her so badly she could taste it.

"Should I add another punishment because you can't keep quiet?" he said in that dominating tone that told her she was about to be in big trouble if she didn't shut her mouth.

She shook her head.

"I might punish you anyway." He tugged on the chain linking one nipple to the other and she had to bite her lower lip hard not to cry out again. "You'll now subjugate to me."

Teri didn't have a chance to wonder what he meant before he held one hand to her belly and pressed on her back with his other while he guided her down. He positioned her so that one cheek was to the floor, her breasts brushed the carpet, and her ass was high in the air. He moved behind her and pushed her knees farther apart so that her thighs were spread wide and her folds and ass were completely bared. Her hands were still cuffed behind her back, and there was no way in hell she could move. And she couldn't see a damn thing.

She thought about shouting her safe word, but she was so turned on that she was sure she could come with a brush against her clit. Maybe he'd drive into her and fuck her just like this. The thought alone made her writhe.

When he had her situated, he moved away from her, and she heard rustling noises, like he was digging in his duffel bag. In the next moment he was behind her and pressing something long and hard inside her pussy—a dildo or a vibrator.

This time she bit the inside of her cheek to keep from making sounds of surprise and pleasure.

"You've been a bad girl, Teri." His warm hand rested on her ass, and he began squeezing one butt cheek and then the other. "You'll learn to obey me in every way. To do what I want *when* I want. Do you understand?"

Teri nodded, her cheek rubbing against the carpet with her movement.

"Good." He moved away again and she heard a squishy sort of sound. "You're getting two punishments at once. If you're not careful you'll get another." Something cool and slick pressed against her anus.

He couldn't. He *wouldn't*.

He did.

Josh slowly slid something deep into her anus, something rubbery slicked with cool gel. Even though he went slow, it stretched her. It hurt. It burned. But like the clamps on her nipples, the pain gradually became pleasure. She felt so incredibly horny, so full, that she couldn't imagine being anywhere but here at this very moment. She wanted him to fuck her just like this.

"My cock is going to be in your ass instead of the plug soon," he said as if he'd heard her thoughts. "Have you ever been fucked in the ass before?"

Her throat already felt rusty. "No, Master."

He moved away again and Teri felt both fear and excitement rise up within her. "The blindfold, the cuffs, the nipple clamps, the dildo, the butt plug, and the flogger will be perfect," he said. "But first let's play with the violet wand."

Teri shivered in anticipation and from sheer nerves. Was he going to shock her? Or let her feel the fizzy, enjoyable sensation?

Yeah, right. Like he'd give her a break. He was going to shock the hell out of her and she knew it.

She couldn't see Josh, but she was aware of him moving away from her before he was back again and she heard the sound of him rustling in that case and the soft snap of something being attached. "You're going to like this."

Sure she would. Teri bit the inside of her lower lip, her whole body rigid until he slid a different attachment across her skin. This one felt thin and like a small roller as he coasted it down one of her ass cheeks. It was a pleasant tingling feeling and she relaxed. A little.

"Do you like it?" Josh said in a voice that sounded like trouble. He was up to something, no doubt about it.

The feel of the wand had actually been good. Really good. Carpet scrubbed her face as she nodded in response to his question. She was afraid to say anything.

He drew it down her other ass cheek and she barely kept herself from wiggling from the sensations that traveled through her body like little prickles of heat. Then he slid it across the lips of her folds and she shivered. God, it felt good and made her want to come so badly she had to fight to pull herself away from climaxing.

"Does this make you want to come?" She imagined the wicked look in Josh's eyes as he spoke.

She nodded again.

"Let's try something different." Josh moved away and her body started to quiver. What was he going to do next?

Oh, she knew exactly—

An incredible jolt shocked her as he pressed the next attach-ment at the nape of her neck. She almost jumped out of her skin and cried "Josh!" But she didn't want to add to the torture, no matter how exquisite.

Teri's eyes watered as he pressed the violet wand intermittently down her spine and she shivered and tried not to writhe and squirm. Every shock sent wild, harsh sensations throughout her body to the point she swore her hair was rising on her scalp and her arms.

He reached under her with the wand and pressed it to her navel before sliding it down her belly to her mound. "You'd better not climax, Teri. I have a good whip and that'll hurt a lot more than the flogger."

Bastard. More tears wet the blindfold. Not from true pain or fear, but from the stimulation that made her feel totally out of control. And like her body wasn't her own anymore.

He gave her a shock against her slit and she couldn't hold back a cry. *Damn him, damn him, damn him.* How could he not let her climax and do this to her?

"You're going to pay for that, slave." Her whole body tensed. "Now for the real lesson." He pressed something firm yet soft and round against her lips. "This is a ball gag to help you hold back your screams."

Her body still tingled from the violet wand and her heart thumped like crazy as he forced the ball into her mouth. How could she shout her safe word now?

Then he pressed a piece of cloth into her hand. "Since you can't speak, here's a scarf. If you want me to stop and end every-thing, drop the scarf."

Some relief trickled through Teri, even though her fear was at its highest of the evening. So far. She nodded.

He again trailed the flogger over her ass. "When I say it'll end, Teri, I mean it'll end. The moment you drop the handkerchief, the moment you say your safe word, I'll send you back to your hotel room."

Teri felt a strange sense of loss at that thought. Like she wanted this. Needed this. She was so close to coming, with her pussy and ass filled, her nipples aching from the clamps, and her body wide open and exposed to him in this position.

"Relax," he murmured as he rubbed her buttocks. "It's going to hurt a lot more if you tense up."

She tried to relax, she really did, but her whole body was like a coiled spring.

"One more thing." He reached under her and pulled on the chain between the nipple clamps, and she gave a moan behind the ball gag. "You can't come without my permission."

Damn.

The flogger tickled her ass as he trailed the soft strands over her skin. The feel of it was soothing and erotic.

But then one lash hit her, and another. She shouted her surprise, but it was muffled by the ball. Her ass cheeks burned, but she grew wetter.

A lash landed harder, and she screamed against the ball gag. This one *really* burned. It hurt so bad tears flooded her eyes behind the blindfold. She almost let go of the scarf that she was gripping tight. Another lash fell, this one right at the spot between the butt plug and the dildo. Again the burn, but this time pleasure hummed along her skin, too.

"Will you be good now, slave?" he said as another lash hit her. She nodded. *Yes, yes, yes!* She'd do whatever he wanted.

But he flogged her over and over, each lash landing in a different area, never the same place twice. How could it feel so good?

The need to climax was building up so intensely within her that she clenched her pussy tight around the dildo, as if that might keep her from coming.

But the more lashes that fell, the more she needed to reach orgasm. She wanted to beg him to stop, but the ball gag was in her mouth and she couldn't tell him she was close to climax.

Her legs trembled so badly she was afraid they might slide out from under her. Surely he knew she was close.

He landed another lash to the place between the dildo and the butt plug, and she lost it.

Her orgasm rocketed through her body. Her channel clenched and unclenched around the dildo, and her anus throbbed around the butt plug. Fire licked her body and she trembled so badly that her legs did give out, and she slipped so that she was flat on her belly. Her body continued to buck and shake until finally the last wave vanished.

It was the best orgasm she'd ever experienced in her life.

Josh moved and yanked off her blindfold. The light seemed so bright now.

She squinted and blinked. When she rolled just enough to see his handsome face her heart nearly stopped beating at his angry expression.

"That was a big mistake." He reached beneath her and tugged on the chain that pulled on her nipple clamps, causing her to cry out behind the ball gag. "Now you'll get a *real* punishment."

Chapter 4

When he was out of Teri's range of sight, Josh smiled in satisfaction. She was the perfect submissive. He didn't know anything about this woman other than the fact that she was a corporate lawyer, she had family in Minneapolis and lived in Los Angeles, and the fact that—although she might be new to BDSM—she was born for it.

Josh reached around and removed the ball gag from her mouth, and she gave a shuddering sigh of relief. He slipped the slick dildo from her pussy. He considered taking out the butt plug, but decided to keep her on edge. She had another punishment on its way, and he planned to make it one she'd never forget. Hell, this night was one she'd never forget, and neither would he.

He left the leather cuffs on her wrists as well, keeping her arms bound behind her back. He helped her ease up from the floor onto her haunches. Her green eyes were dilated, her lips wide and inviting, and one cheek was red from being against the carpet.

And her back, thighs, and buttocks were covered with his marks. Light pink stripes that looked beautiful against her pale skin.

He tugged on the silver chain between the clamps, and she bit her lip hard to keep from crying out. Her engorged nipples needed circulation, and he unclamped one after the other. He knew she'd feel a moment of intense pain before pleasure and relief. The watering of her eyes and the intensity of her expression told him he was right.

He brushed a tear from her eye with his thumb. "You always have your safe word."

She nodded, but said nothing.

His slave for the night was so beautiful, and his cock was so damn hard. He stood in front of her, unfastened his belt, and opened his jeans to set his cock and balls free. Teri's eyes widened and her lips parted.

"Let's see how well you give head, slave." Josh gripped her hair and brought her to his erection. He forced himself between her lips and slid to the back of her throat. She gagged a little, but began sucking him off. Damn, but her mouth felt so good around his cock. "Yeah, that's it, slave. I'm going to fuck your mouth before your next punishment."

Josh kept his grip on her hair, keeping her still as he thrust his cock in and out of her mouth. He was careful not to go too deep, not wanting to hurt her. The pressure, the need to come was unbelievable. "Look at me," he demanded when she lowered her gaze.

She made him want to come *now* as he watched the wide green eyes that were focused on him. Seeing his wet cock sliding in and out of her beautiful lips brought him that much closer to climax. To have this powerful woman on her knees before him was such a turn on.

He fucked her mouth faster, the orgasm building within him so great that he ground his teeth. "I'm going to come on your breasts," he said and pulled his cock out of her mouth just before he lost it. His balls drew up and an intense sensation burst from his sac to the head of his cock. His fluid jetted onto her breasts. His body jerked as each spasm of his climax rolled through him.

When he had spent himself, he was breathing hard and a bead of sweat trickled down the side of his forehead. He wiped it away on his shoulder, then tucked his cock back into his jeans and zipped up. He took Teri by her upper arms and drew her up to stand before him.

At that moment he wanted to kiss her so badly, to taste her mouth as much as he wanted to taste her pussy. But he was waiting. Making *her* wait.

"Did you enjoy sucking me off, slave?" Josh said as he trailed one of his fingers through the sticky fluid on her breasts.

She nodded, and he could see the honesty in her eyes.

He gripped her by the arm and led her to the bedroom. She looked so incredibly sexy, naked and only in high heels, his collar, and the leather cuffs.

After he wiped his fluid from her chest, with a wet cloth from the bathroom, he said, "Lie on your belly on the bed. And don't move."

Josh had to help her scoot up so that she was facedown in the middle of the bed. He paused to admire his handiwork again and could just imagine how the sting on her backside was making her feel. No doubt her orgasm had left her feeling raw and on edge, and anything he did to her now was going to make it even more difficult for her not to come a second time without his permission.

He left her on the bed to move to his special suitcase full of tools of what he considered to be his craft, in addition to what he'd had in the duffel bag. He was an artist when it came to BDSM, turning his slaves into works of art, and no matter where he traveled he took a good amount of his tools with him, in case he went to a BDSM club and met a beautiful woman looking for a Dom. He hadn't expected someone like Teri, though.

The leather straps he needed were neatly folded to one side of the suitcase. When he returned to Teri, her eyes widened at the sight of the long strips of leather that had buckles on one end and clamps on the other. He didn't bother to tell her what they were for. Instead he fastened each of the leather straps around the lower legs of the bed. It wasn't a four-poster, of course, so he needed another method of restraint.

Teri remained quiet as he worked, but he saw how hard she was breathing by the movement of her back. He smelled her rich musk and the scent of her skin mixed with her plumeria perfume. Her dark hair was loose and wild around her shoulders, and her green eyes were wide as she turned her cheek to the bedspread and watched him.

After he was done attaching the restraints to each leg of the bed, he grabbed a couple of ankle cuffs. Starting with one ankle, he cuffed her, then hooked a leg restraint to it and tightened it so that she couldn't move. In moments he had her other leg fastened. After unhooking her wrists, he moved them from behind her back and fastened them to the leather straps at the front bedposts.

When he finished restraining his new plaything, he stopped to look in satisfaction at her beautiful body spread out upon the bed. Her legs were spread so wide that her folds and clit were well exposed to him, as well as the butt plug that was still up her ass.

"Good girl," he murmured as he rubbed her flogged ass with

his hand and felt her tremble beneath his touch. Her skin was smooth to his callused palm, but he felt the warmth from the strokes he had given her. Just touching her and seeing her that way made his cock grow hard again.

He turned away from her and headed for the suite's bar and refrigerator.

Teri didn't know whether to laugh or cry. All she knew was that she was being erotically tortured, she'd had the most incredible orgasm of her life, she'd just given him head, and it had turned her on to see him spill his semen on her chest.

And now here she was, strapped facedown on the bed, spread-eagle. She was just as open and vulnerable as she had been when he had her on her knees, face to the floor and blindfolded.

Her skin tingled when Josh walked away, his footsteps muffled by the carpeting. How was he going to torture her next? Would he whip her this time? Oh, God, would it hurt?

What he'd done to her so far—it had been incredible. She never would have believed she'd enjoy sexual pain, but she had. It had actually been *pleasurable*.

She'd wanted to fuck a stranger, and she'd definitely gotten more than she'd bargained for.

When Josh returned, he came up beside her to where she could see him. He was carrying an ice bucket and a bottle that looked like champagne. He set the champagne bottle and a cork remover on the nightstand, along with a few foil packets.

Her heart thudded. He wasn't planning on fucking her just once.

He took the ice bucket with him as he moved behind her and

out of her range of sight. "You're going to tell me about yourself, slave," Josh said as the bed sank beneath his weight. He was sitting between her splayed thighs. "I want to know everything about you while you receive your punishment."

Well, that was the last thing she'd expected. "Yes, Master." She licked her lips as she anticipated what he was going to do next. "What do you want to know?"

"How about your childhood?" he said, just before she felt something so cold against her ass that she had to choke down a cry.

It had to be ice that he was stroking her buttocks with. The freezing chunk of ice contrasted with the burn she still felt from the flogging. It gave her a different sort of pain and pleasure.

"I—" She gasped as he circled the butt plug with the ice and paused at the sensitive area between her pussy and her anus. "Um, I was born in San Diego."

Cold water from melted ice dripped down her body. "Tell me about your family."

Well, what could it hurt? If they could be this intimate, she could share a little about her history. "My dad left me and my mom and sister when I was just a kid," she said, "and I never saw him again. I lived in San Diego until I was eighteen then went to UCLA, and my mom passed away just a couple of years later."

She paused and made a hissing sound as he stroked the crevice between her thigh and pussy with the ice. "What next?" he asked.

"When I—I passed the bar exam, I went straight to work for the firm I'm with n-now." She was having a *really* hard time talking, the way he was trailing the cube down the inside of one thigh, to the back of her knee, and down her calf to her ankle. "I do a lot of traveling, Master."

Josh slipped off her high heel just before he ran the ice cube along the arch of her foot. She couldn't help giggling when it tickled her, or stop herself from jerking her ankle against the restraints. She thought she heard amusement in his voice when he added, "Now I know you're ticklish." He moved to her other foot, flipped off her shoe, and ran the ice down her arch, causing her to giggle and squirm again. "Very ticklish. I wonder where else?"

She wasn't about to tell him that. Not until he said, "Tell me, slave. I'll know you're lying if you don't tell me the truth. Where are you ticklish?"

Ah, man. "My knees and my underarms, Master."

She heard the shift of ice against ice in the bucket, and then he was applying a bigger piece to her leg. She shivered from the cold, and her body ached so badly to be fucked. This waiting, the way he was drawing it out, the ice freezing and biting her skin and melting—all of it was driving her crazy.

"What about *you*, I want to know more," he said as he reached the inside of her other thigh.

"Well . . ." Jeez, what was there to her other than her job? "I don't really have any kind of social life. I don't know my neighbors, and like I told you, I don't have any pets." Her voice shook as he reached her folds. "I guess I'm boring, Master."

"I think you're anything but, slave," he said, just as he pressed an ice cube against her clit.

Teri cried out at the extreme sensation of ice against her sensitive flesh. *Oh. My. God.* Her clit was on fire, it was so cold. He held it there and the fire turned into a cold numbness that had her trembling.

"What makes you tick?" He forced the ice tighter against her clit. "Not your job, not material things. What's inside of you?"

She was having a really hard time focusing on his question. When the words finally came out, they surprised her. "I—I'm outwardly forward, but inside I'm really hesitant. I don't make friends easily."

"Why do you think that is?" he said.

For some reason it felt freeing to tell this stranger her deepest feelings. "It's because I'm afraid of . . . rejection."

He moved the ice cube away from her clit and her muscles went slack with relief. She heard the ice bucket again, and then he stuck a large, smooth piece right at the entrance to her core.

Oh, God. Again the sensitive flesh around the opening was on fire and hurriedly becoming cold, then numb. Her pussy clenched and unclenched around the ice.

"You're afraid of commitment, too," he stated as he pushed the ice in deeper. "That's why the thought of fucking a stranger appeals to you."

That familiar heat rose to her cheeks despite the cold. She swallowed as she fought off the sensations the ice was creating in her body. It was barely inside her, yet she felt it all the way to her belly.

"I guess so, Master," she mumbled. "I travel too much, and, well, it's just easier this way."

"And you don't have to worry about anyone leaving you, or dying on you."

The bluntness of his statement overwhelmed her. Was that why she shied away from relationships? Because she'd been hurt too many times?

"Teri . . ." he said with a strong note of warning in his tone, surprising her by using her name instead of "slave."

"Yes, Master," she said quietly.

"Good girl." He moved the ice from her pussy up to her anus, where the butt plug was still filling her. "Would you like me to fuck you now, Teri?"

"Yes, Master." Teri shivered again from the cold of the ice.

"I'm not finished with your punishment."

Chapter 5

Josh got up and moved away, and Teri almost banged her head against the bed in frustration. This man was drawing out her erotic torture the same way he was drawing out the darkest thoughts from the depths of her soul.

When he returned he was out of her line of vision still, so she didn't know what he had planned this time. He removed the butt plug and she felt an aching emptiness. But then he shoved something much larger into her anus, and she screamed in surprise and pain.

She choked back a sob as her body conformed to the larger butt plug, and it didn't surprise her this time when she began to enjoy the sensation of it being deep in her ass. Even the burning from its entry didn't bother her after a few moments.

Josh came up beside her and grabbed the bottle of champagne from the nightstand, opened it, and raised the bottle over her back. Slowly he poured little splashes along her spine, over her buttocks, and down into her folds.

Teri's reaction was immediate. She cried out and thrashed against her bonds from the feel of the champagne bubbles and the cool fluid. She moaned and shivered as Josh began to flick his tongue along her spine, slowly licking up the champagne.

She discovered she had another ticklish spot—right at the base of her spine. Then he lapped her folds and she squirmed.

He took the end of the butt plug in his hand and thrust it in and out of her ass a few times as he moved his mouth near her folds.

Teri trembled all over from the feel of his tongue along her skin, the butt plug fucking her ass, and now his mouth so close to her pussy.

"Mmmm, champagne and woman," he said just before he buried his mouth against her pussy.

"Josh!" she cried out as his tongue began to lap her folds. He paused and she hurried to say, "Master, I mean Master."

He gave an approving rumble, and began licking and sucking at her folds. He paused only long enough to say, "Don't come without permission, slave. Remember that."

Teri moaned. She was so close, so turned on, so out of control. She jerked against her restraints and writhed beneath his tongue. She'd get so close, and then he'd back off before starting the torture again, as if he sensed her body's needs. The smells of sex, of champagne, of Josh's masculine scent, enhanced every sensation.

The pain of the flogging, the ache from the nipple clamps, the intense feeling of the butt plug—all of it added together to make her completely crazy with desire.

She was sure, so sure, she couldn't take it anymore when he

finally stopped. Sweat rolled down her cheeks, she was covered in perspiration, and the sheet was damp and cool against her skin from the melted ice. Her whole body trembled.

He moved to his suitcase again, and this time he brought back a leash and clipped it to the D ring on her collar, then let the leather lie along her back, nestled in her ass crack. He stood at the head of the bed, by her face. His icy gray eyes studied her as he unfastened his pants again and released his cock and balls. *Damn*, did he have a nice cock—she'd really enjoyed giving him head.

He tore open one of the foil packets and sheathed his erection with it. Her anticipation grew as he moved behind her and between her splayed legs. She felt his hands at each ankle just before he released the restraints. Her legs were free.

"Move so that you're on your knees," he commanded, but he helped her at the same time. Her arms were still stretched out, and one cheek was against the bed.

When her ass was high in the air she trembled with excitement. He was finally going to fuck her. She'd finally feel him deep inside.

He removed the butt plug and tossed it onto the floor. Before she had a chance to take a breath, he drove his lubed cock into her ass.

Teri screamed. Fire, burning, then pleasure as he began to pump in and out of her. He grabbed the leash and forced her head up as he took her in the ass. It was uncomfortable having her head pulled up, but she was so lost in the moment she didn't care. He fucked her long and hard, reaching a spot inside her that she'd never known could be so pleasurable.

"That's it, slave." Josh slammed his hips harder against hers, his balls slapping her. "Take my cock. Take me deep inside your ass."

· · ·

It took all Josh had to pull out before he came. He wanted to delay his own orgasm.

Damn, this woman was sexy. She just might be what he'd been missing. He'd had lots of sexy women before, but intuition told him there was something special about Teri.

He released the leash and let her head loll forward. She was breathing hard and her body glistened with sweat.

After Josh climbed off the bed and disposed of the condom so that he could use a fresh one in her pussy, he unfastened the wrist restraints and removed her cuffs. The only thing he left on her was his metal-studded collar.

"On your back, bend your knees, and keep your legs open wide," he ordered.

Teri obeyed, and when she was settled he took the opportunity to view her beautiful body. Her skin was flushed, her green eyes dark with desire, her brown hair in a silken mass against the white sheets.

He left her for a moment, then returned with two champagne glasses. He reached for the champagne bottle and poured what was left into the glasses. But rather than offer one to Teri or take a drink himself he left the glasses on the nightstand. He moved between her thighs and slid the neck of the bottle into her pussy, and gently started fucking her with it.

She cried out and grasped the bedsheet with her hands, her knuckles whitening.

"Do you like this, slave?" Josh asked, keeping his eyes always on Teri, watching her for any signs of discomfort. "Do you want me to keep fucking you with the bottle?"

"Yes." Teri moaned with every impact of the champagne bottle. "But I'd rather have *you* fuck me, Master."

Frankly, he couldn't wait any longer. His control had been tested to the limit. He tossed aside the bottle and it landed with a thump on the carpet. In just a matter of moments he'd stripped out of his clothing and stood at the foot of the bed, his cock hard and ready to take her.

Teri took in Josh's naked, athletic body. He was muscular, fit, and so damn good-looking. She took all of him in, from his blond hair to his ice gray eyes, broad shoulders, trim hips, and athletic thighs.

Her pussy was drenched from all the erotic torture and her nipples still ached from the clamps. Her backside burned from the flogger, yet she felt chilled from the ice. It all combined to make her so incredibly horny that all she could think about was Josh's cock in her.

Josh took a moment to sheathe himself with a fresh condom and then he was back between her legs. He grasped her hips and drew her down so that her ass was resting on the edge of the bed and her knees were bent close to her chest. Her breathing quickened as he pressed his hips between her thighs and his gray eyes held hers.

He lowered his torso so that his hands were braced to either side of her shoulders, and his face was close to hers. "You make a very good slave." He brushed his lips lightly over hers, and it tickled her lips when he said, "Have you liked being my plaything?"

"Yes, Master," she whispered just before his mouth took hers. After all they had done together tonight, this was the first time he had kissed her. And God, what a kiss. It was a gentle exploration, not the forceful domination she'd expected. He tasted so good. Of male and champagne, and her, too. He bit her lower lip, just hard enough to make her sigh.

When he rose up he kept his gaze fixed on hers. He positioned his cock at her entrance, sliding in just a fraction, just enough to make her squirm in anticipation. She needed him deeper, needed him *now*. He hooked his arms under her knees, raised her up high, and drove his cock into her.

Teri cried out at the exquisite sensation of him thrusting in and out of her. The way he was holding her, the way he was looking at her—this was not a Dom and his slave. This was a man and a woman. He seemed almost . . . tender.

He took her long and slow, and she gripped the sheets to anchor herself. He filled her so perfectly, so thick, so long.

She drew closer and closer to climax.

"Squeeze your nipples," he said in a husky voice that didn't sound like a command. It sounded more like desire, like he needed to see what she looked like when she touched herself.

Teri brought her hands up to her breasts and cupped them before she pinched her nipples and gave a loud moan. They were still sore from the nipple clamps, but the added sensation of her squeezing them while she was being fucked made her wild for her orgasm.

Higher and higher she climbed. It was like she was flying. She was ready to beg him to let her come. He took her harder, then harder yet. Faster, and faster yet.

When her thighs started quivering in his arms and she knew she was almost to the point of no return, Josh thrust even deeper into her. "Come for me, Teri," he said gently. "Yes, honey, come for me."

Her orgasm slammed into her like a tidal wave. It was like she was being turned inside out and then back again. Josh kept pumping in and out of her until he shouted and his cock throbbed inside her. Every pulse of his cock matched the contractions inside her channel.

Finally, he released her legs and withdrew his cock. He tossed the spent condom aside, then caught her up to him so that her thighs were clamped around his waist and he was carrying her from the bottom edge to the side of the bed. With a groan of satisfaction, he rolled them both onto the mattress and arranged them so that his body spooned hers. She snuggled into his embrace and gave a long, relaxed sigh.

Being fucked by a stranger had never felt so good.

Chapter 6

Teri grabbed her two-piece fitted suit for the final day of negotiations. During the week she'd spent her days negotiating contracts at the corporation. . . .

And her nights at Josh's mercy. A whole week of insane pleasure.

After the second night together they had moved all of her things to his room, and she had given complete control over to him—in the bedroom. She wasn't a lifestyle sub, and didn't think she could be. But God, how she loved it in the bedroom.

While she fastened her garters, Teri relived that first night they'd been together, after they'd fallen asleep. They had awoken during the night and Josh entered her, treating her gently, like a fragile object, even though he knew just how rough she'd enjoyed it earlier. After she came in yet another spectacular orgasm, they snuggled together once again.

Only this time they talked into the early hours of the morning.

By the time they had each ended up spilling everything about themselves to each other Teri had been drained. She fell asleep, still in his arms, and happier than she could remember being in a long time.

Teri smiled as the skirt of her suit slid over her naked ass. She'd taken to not wearing underwear while spending these wonderful days with Josh. She felt wicked when she was making presentations and handling negotiations in a roomful of mostly men. As always she was a professional—tough, and sometimes intimidating. But underneath, her pussy remained damp, and she couldn't wait to get back to the hotel and Josh.

During the day, Josh attended and made presentations at the conference he'd come for. The conference was related to the stock brokerage firm he owned.

She put on the fitted suited jacket and frowned as she slipped the last button through its hole. Tomorrow she was scheduled to fly to New York City. Tonight would be her last night with Josh.

Would he want to see her again, when she was home in Los Angeles?

She'd only known the man a week, but she hated the idea of not seeing Josh again. At the thought of never being near him once they left the hotel, she accidentally jabbed her scalp with the clip as she put her hair up.

Tears moistened her eyes from the pain and she let the clip drop to the countertop in the suite's opulent bathroom. She gazed into the mirror, seeing this time a woman who was well rested and very satisfied. Had it been only a week ago that she'd stared at her exhausted face's reflection, knowing she needed something else in her life?

"Teri," came Josh's voice from the bedroom, jarring her from her thoughts.

Her heart beat a little faster at the sound of his voice, and it pushed aside any thoughts of sadness at their parting.

When she reached the bedroom, her heart thudded even more. Josh was holding a bouquet of yellow roses with sprigs of baby's breath. Her favorite color. Instead of a dominant look on his features, he looked almost boyish, hopeful.

She took the roses from him, inhaled their sweet fragrance, then looked back at Josh. "Thank you," she said, and then noticed he was holding a long, flat, navy blue velvet box.

Her pulse rate kicked up. Josh took the bouquet from her hands and set it on the vanity table. When her hands were free, he placed the velvet box in them.

"Open it," he said in a husky voice as she stood and stared at it.

She swallowed and lifted the lid, and caught her breath. Inside was what looked like a choker made from triple strands of fine gold. Gold-and-diamond bars were positioned around the choker, holding the three strands together.

When she raised her head, her gaze met his gray eyes. She'd never seen the look on his features that he had right now. Uncertainty.

"I want to see you again, Teri." He reached up and cupped her face in his hand. "Whenever you're at home in LA, I want to be with you and to give us a chance to get to know each other better." He dropped his gaze to the choker before meeting her eyes again. "This is a collar I had specially designed for you. If you agree to continue our relationship, I'd like you to wear it."

Without giving a moment's thought, Teri flung her arms around Josh's neck. "Yes," she murmured against his chest. "Yes to everything."

He drew back and took the box from her hands. While she watched, he slipped the collar from the box, then set the box aside. He brought the collar to her neck, and she lifted her hair so that he could fasten it.

It settled around her throat perfectly. He turned her so that she was facing the vanity mirror, and she brought her fingers up to trace the strands. "It's beautiful, Josh."

He took her by the shoulders and brushed his lips over hers. "*You're* beautiful."

Josh maneuvered her so that she was sitting on the edge of the bed. She was already in tune with his thoughts and hiked up her skirt to reveal her bare mound. At the same time he unzipped his slacks and released his cock.

After putting on a condom, he slid into her wet channel, taking her in a way that he'd never taken her before. Slow and sensual, with need and a sweet urgency.

His thrusts became deeper and harder, and she rose up to meet every plunge.

Her orgasm came out of nowhere. She gave a cry and her body trembled beneath his. He thrust into her several times more before groaning with his own release.

The moment they could both catch their breath, Josh smiled at Teri. "You've just earned another punishment."

Teri smiled back. She couldn't wait.

Take a sneak peek at Cheyenne McCray's
debut urban fantasy novel

Demons Not Included

Coming Summer 2009
St. Martin's Paperbacks

Olivia, T, and I arrived at almost the same time to the Upper East Side Manhattan neighborhood where the NYPD officer's family had been murdered. We parked a distance from the home—couldn't get any closer due to the large number of emergency vehicles.

At least four police cruisers, three ambulances, a fire truck, and two unmarked vehicles had already arrived at the scene. Standing outside the fringes of the crime scene tape and police barricades were neighbors, most still in their bathrobes.

Everyone and everything was motionless. Frozen.

Thanks to a Soothsayer's power to control air and the minute water particles in it, the moment an onlooker happened by, that person instantly "froze," too. The Soothsayer also would use an air spell to put a glamour over the entire block.

Of course the spells excluded paranorms.

A strange scent came from the house and I grimaced as Olivia,

T, and I walked toward the scene. Burned flesh and the additional sickly sweet scent of burned sugar assaulted our noses.

I'd seen dead bodies before—lots of them—but with each step I took, my back and arms felt tighter. I had to bite my bottom lip to hold back a powerful retch.

There was more here than dead bodies. Something else. Something . . .

Evil?

I shivered as I walked. Tried to remind myself that there was no such division as good and evil. Only dark and light, and all the shades in between—but that was my Drow mind talking. The human part of me definitely wanted to scream and run away from this place.

Crime scene tape remained as motionless as the people. We made it to the front door of the home after dodging our way through motionless NYPD officers, an FDNY response unit, paramedics, and on past crime scene investigators, including a photographer and a sketch artist. Our Soothsayer would have to take care of them later when she wiped their memories of the paranormal parts of the crimes.

The lurch of my heart was no less painful than the churning in the pit of my belly when I saw four body bags outside the home and two of them were small.

The moment I entered the home, the stench hit me even harder—along with a sick, slithering feeling of something wrong, something unnatural and more terrible than I could put into words.

Olivia came up beside me. "Here comes Tinkerbell."

Great. The Soothsayer standing away from a chalk outline was Lulu and she flexed her fingers at the sight of me and Olivia.

I was so not in the mood to be frozen.

I looked around what was apparently the living room. Experts had been dusting for fingerprints while other police officers were obviously looking for clues.

And there was Adam, frozen in a crouch, his back to me, his muscles tight, radiating a bleak, gut-tearing energy I had never felt from him before.

My heart immediately started pounding from excitement at the sight of him, and from worry. I left T and Olivia behind and went to Adam and crouched beside him.

He wouldn't know I was there until I touched him, but I could see pain in those gorgeous blue eyes and that made my chest ache.

His expression told me everything I needed to know.

These were his people, a cop's family. He was taking this as personally as I took the death of a fellow Tracker.

I braced one knee on the polished wood floor and I touched the sleeve of Adam's worn leather bomber jacket, unfreezing him. "Adam," I whispered, overcome by his sadness.

"This blue looks like fresh paint—" Adam stopped and glanced at me. "Nyx."

He seemed both pleased to see me, yet angry at what had happened. I gave him a sad smile.

Adam moved his gaze to the man on the other side of him, who was still frozen. "Christ, I wish your Soothsayers wouldn't do this freezing sh— crap. It makes everything harder."

When he shifted his weight from one knee to the other, I caught his leather-coffee-and-masculine scent, and wanted to wrap my arms around him. I leaned closer so that I could breathe more of him in, and hope that he might take comfort from my presence.

He looked around and saw Lulu, who had her hands on her hips. Humans were the lowest of creatures as far as she was concerned.

T came up and crouched on the other side of me. I worked to keep my attention fully on Adam to let him know I was there for him, that I understood how bad this kind of thing felt.

A few moments later, I felt T's awareness turn to Adam, too, and Adam's turned to T.

They did that male sizing-up thing, and Adam's tension seemed to rise. I almost rolled my eyes for the second time since coming to the liaison officer's home.

"Boyd." Adam got to his feet and held out his hand to T.

"Torin." With a slight nod, T stood at the same time I did, then he reached across me and shook hands with Adam.

"Definitely a paranormal crime," Adam said to me after he and T released their grips. "You won't believe some of the shit we found." He gestured toward what I knew wasn't paint, but blue blood. "This isn't the half of it. Think it could be those Demons you were telling me about?"

I took a good look around me. "I don't think that underling Demons could possibly do this."

"Why not?" Adam said.

"After fighting the underling Demons for a while, I just can't picture it." The total destruction of the home was almost overwhelming. "The power it would have taken to do this is like a cyclone was contained within this house."

"Could be the major or master Demons that Rodán told you about." Olivia gripped her electro-pad in one hand. "No one knows what they're capable of. Yet."

I made an absent-minded sound of acknowledgment as I caught sight of more blue spots. They were on carpet that lay over a portion of the wood floor. "The Demons do have blue blood and there are more scattered droplets." I pointed. "Right there."

"Not paint, huh?" Adam asked as we walked toward the spots of blue that hadn't fully dried.

"It's possible the major Demons or master Demon also have that same color of blood," T said.

"Did your Proctor tell you anything?" Adam cleared his throat. "Do you think Officer Crisman was, uh, eaten or something?"

"It *is* possible but we really don't know," I said. "Hopefully we'll find more clues than this blue stuff."

Somewhere in my purse was my electro-pad where I kept my notes on every case. I dug through my purse and came up with it. Adam watched me as I jotted down a few notes with the stylus.

I looked up at Adam. My human-half didn't like to ask these kinds of questions. "Were the bodies mutilated?"

It was obvious to me that Adam was trying to keep his professional-cop cool. "Their faces are—hell, I don't know what you'd call it. Mutilated and burned off would be the closest thing I can come up with."

"Goddess." I glanced to T, who frowned. I moved my gaze back to Adam's. "That's definitely not underling Demon behavior."

T shook his head in a slight movement, his frown deepening. "Impossible."

"So you think we're probably dealing with another type of Demon or Demons," Adam said.

"Right now the only thing I know for sure is that a Tracker and a human law enforcement officer were attacked the same night, in the same vicinity," I said. I didn't want to ask, but I had to. "May I see one of the bodies?"

Adam studied me. "They're pretty bad."

"I need to get a look at them." I rubbed my fingers lightly over my Drow collar, which always gave me a burst of strength and confidence when I needed it. "Olivia and I need to." I glanced at T. "Oh, and him, too."

T scowled.

Adam started toward the body bags. "I know you've seen some pretty crappy things, Nyx, but this—like I said, it's bad."

"Stop babying her," Olivia said as she came toward us with her electro-pad and stylus gripped tight. "She needs toughening up."

As if.

Adam nodded and I walked beside him to the largest of the bags. "From the ID he was carrying, apparently this is the grandfather."

He inched down the zipper. A very much human gag reflex came over me as I breathed in the even stronger smell of burned sugar and flesh.

And saw the face—or what was left of the man's face.

It wasn't as if the flesh had been seared—no part of the skull was exposed. Instead, it was like something had taken a big stamp and flattened the flesh so that the face looked like a wax blob and not a human face.

A shock went through my elemental energies, nearly stealing from me my ability to breathe. The haze in my mind was like I'd drained nearly all of my powers.

"Holy shit," Olivia said.

T grunted.

My Drow half was screaming for me to draw blades at the side of it. I could hardly keep my own cool.

"Nyx." Olivia's voice came through the haze in my mind. "What are you sensing?"

"I don't know." I swallowed down the desire to vomit, scream, and run like I've never run before.

Adam said, "I think we'd better get you out of here." The concern in his voice was unmistakable and protective.

Even though I felt my energies draining, I forced myself to study the face. I had to be professional. But all I wanted to do was flee.

Calm down. Calm down, Nyx.

I scanned the horrific image. It took a moment, but then I made it out. A pattern had been "stamped" into the flesh.

"What the hell is that?" Olivia asked but, like Adam, maintained her professional-cop cool.

My gaze traced the strange lines and whirls. I couldn't speak.

T stood. "Let's see the others."

Olivia, T, and I checked the other bodies and each time the human half of me wanted to throw up. Only my Drow half kept me from losing it.

Each face had the same symbol distorting the darkened flesh. A sort of cone or funnel. The symbol was like nothing I'd ever seen.

Pretending that the horrible images I was looking at were just on wax dummies and not on real people, I used my electro-pad to photograph the faces.

I worried that the symbol wouldn't photograph well, in case the Demon had put some kind of spell on the faces, so I used the stylus on a blank screen to copy the pattern.

I started to get up, but what T did next brought me to a complete halt. With slow purpose, he moved his hand over the face of the fourth victim. The nightmarish look of the face vanished and was replaced by what looked like a sleeping child. The bad energy vanished around the child's body.

Oh, my Goddess. I held my hand to my mouth. As I looked at that small angelic-looking girl I would have cried if I could. Whatever T had done made it all the more real.

"Maybe he'll be useful after all," Olivia said.

I watched as T did the same to the other three faces so that they looked normal and human—and peaceful, with their eyes closed.

Even the odor of charred flesh had vanished. Only the smell of burned sugar remained. I no longer felt a hint of the darkness remaining in the bodies, and my own energy started to flow back into me.

I stared at T for a moment when he was finished. "How did you do that?"

He studied the room. "We should start looking for clues."

Adam and I exchanged looks.

"Thank you," Adam said to T. "It would have been pretty damned bad for their extended families to see them that way."

We had to dodge police officers and others as we searched for any kind of clues. I walked slowly around the house, checking each room.

Then I found it.

"Hey." I stared at the same image that had been on the faces, but it was much clearer on the wood floor of the dining room. It looked like it had been lasered into the wood then painted with blood. Smelled like it, too. "Get over here."

They all reached my side at almost the same time. Adam whistled through his teeth as T and Olivia crouched beside the symbol. I took a few pictures with my electro-pad.

I lowered myself so that one of my knees was on the floor while I used my thigh to brace the pad on so that I could do my best to sketch the symbol again, this time a lot more clearly and with more detail.

The symbol started with a flat, bumpy surface, then spiraled down, like a cone, but was jagged and uneven in what looked like layers.

"What does this thing mean?" Adam asked as he crouched beside me so that all four of us were down, examining the strange symbol.

"Not sure." I shook my head. "I'll have to check with my Proctor to see if he has any idea. Derek, James's partner, is an occult expert. I'll scan and e-mail the image to Derek right away."

I could see Olivia's mind working overtime as she appraised the symbol. "We'll do an Internet search to see if we come up with a match."

"We can check a few symbol books, too," I said. "I have some and Rodán has a good-sized library."

T's voice came from the other side of me. "We have more on our hands than random acts by a rogue Demon."

A chill ran through me even though I'd been thinking the same thing. All I could do was nod.

"I think this Demon is taunting us with this clue," I said as I shut off my electro-pad and stuffed it into my purse.

T's strong features seemed strangely impassive. "It wants to let us know what it can do. And maybe that it can't be stopped."

Adam was brave and I didn't want him to get hurt.

But this time I wasn't sure I could stop him from avenging these deaths. And if I tried, he would probably never forgive me. But we were dealing with a Demon. What looked like a powerful Demon. A master Demon.

A gut feeling told me this Demon was playing with us and that a timer had started to count down.

Tick. Tick. Tick.

The Demon had given us a bizarre symbol that we had to decipher.

Before we ran out of time.

For Cheyenne's Readers

Be sure to go to http://cheyennemccray.com to sign up for her *private* book announcement list and get *free exclusive* Cheyenne McCray goodies. Please feel free to e-mail her at chey@cheyennemccray.com. She would love to hear from you.

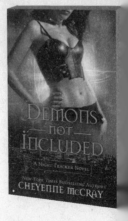